ANNA'S WORLD

ANNA'S WORLD

Marie-Claire Blais

Translated by
SHEILA FISCHMAN

Introduction by
CAMILLA GIBB

Exile Editions

Publishers of singular
Fiction, Poetry, Translation, Drama, Nonfiction and Graphic Books

2009

Library and Archives Canada Cataloguing in Publication

Blais, Marie-Claire, 1939-
[Visions d'Anna, ou, Le vertige. English]
    Anna's world / Marie-Claire Blais ; translated by Sheila Fischman ;
introduction by Camilla Gibb.

Translation of: Visions d'Anna, ou, Le vertige.
Includes bibliographical references.

ISBN 978-1-55096-130-0
    I. Fischman, Sheila II. Title.
PS8503.L33V4813 2009   C843'.54   C2009-905528-7

Design and Composition by Digital ReproSet
Cover Photographs by permission of Creatista ; Sidsnapper / iStockphoto
Typeset in Garamond and Bembo at the Moons of Jupiter Studios
Printed in Canada by Gauvin Imprimerie

The publisher would like to acknowledge the financial assistance of
The Canada Council for the Arts and the Ontario Arts Council.

 Conseil des Arts   Canada Council
du Canada   for the Arts    ONTARIO ARTS COUNCIL
CONSEIL DES ARTS DE L'ONTARIO

Published in Canada in 2009 by Exile Editions Ltd.
144483 Southgate Road 14
General Delivery
Holstein, Ontario, N0G 2A0
info@exileeditions.com
www.ExileEditions.com

Canadian Sales Distribution: U.S. Sales Distribution:
McArthur & Company   Independent Publishers Group
c/o Harper Collins   814 North Franklin Street
1995 Markham Road   Chicago, IL 60610
Toronto, ON M1B 5M8   www.ipgbook.com
toll free: 1 800 387 0117   toll free: 1 800 888 4741

to my goddaughter, Nathalie

INTRODUCTION

Every generation faces its threat of extinction, be it by war, environmental catastrophe or epidemic, but it is, of course, the particular threat that confronts one's own generation that rates as the most acute and potentially devastating in history. For Marie-Claire Blais' Anna, a teenager in the early 1980s, there is famine in Africa, the ozone layer and acid rain to worry about, but above all, it is the heat of the Cold War and the threat of nuclear disaster that make annihilation of the species seem imminent.

I can attest: that fear was palpable. I was fourteen years old the year that *Anna's World* was first published as *Visions d'Anna, ou, Le vertige*, and among my contemporaries it was threat of the bomb that shaped our vision of ourselves and our perception of our fates. We were waiting for World War III, imagining men, always and only men, sitting in desert mountain bunkers with fingers poised on red buttons to be depressed with the inevitable call from the Oval Office.

"Don't go to school, the earth might blow up today," says thirteen-year-old Michelle, to Anna. For Michelle and Anna, "the atomic volcano was there, inhabiting all [their] thoughts." They live "touched by the thin black cloud advancing peacefully towards the earth, slowly, soundlessly, in a great silence, and in a few moments it would snuff out everything that lived." They had "grown up, in terror." As had we all.

Even our approach to sex and sexuality was framed in terms of the bomb (not surprising, perhaps, because sex and sexuality concerned us above all): it seemed of critical importance to lose one's virginity before the end of the world. And so we did, but the world would not end, it would simply slap us with the news that we had been fools. By the time *Anna's World* was published in English in 1985, a strange and localized virus that had first gained attention in 1981 had spread and been renamed HIV. It was AIDS, not the bomb that was going to kill us. Perestroika was on the horizon. The end would not come from some far away place, but in the course of our most intimate exchanges.

Anna's World immediately predates awareness of HIV/ AIDS. The threat to Anna's generation is perceived as mighty, global and removed, the work of the military-industrial complex, the evildoing of "the army of present-day Nazis, the most skilful, the most subtle in our history."

Anna is sixteen, sensitive, intelligent, and preoccupied with her impotence in the face of certain death. Why bother living, one might ask, as both Anna and Michelle do repeatedly, but inertia and despondency, nihilism and anhedonia don't compel one much toward action, even of the suicidal kind. Anna's "one savage passion" is "her desire for such neutrality that any feeling of pain would henceforth be cleansed, expelled from her heart.

Sex, alcohol and drugs are ways to seek that neutrality and Anna and Michelle take what they can wherever they can find it. Michelle refuses, furthermore, to eat or bathe, while Anna repels anyone who gets near her and runs off to the Caribbean for a time hoping to exile herself from her life and family ties.

For Anna, family is principally her mother, Raymonde. Peter, her distant father, is divorced from her mother and has taken up with a new family he would rather not have Anna's presence disturb. Raymonde's longtime friend Guislaine has her own problematic daughters, Michelle and her older sister, the sexually deviant Liliane.

While Guislane's husband is present, he is a thinker, an eminent sociologist who reacts to all with brain rather than heart.

Raymonde's boyfriend, Alexandre, is another man barely there – running off in search of solitude whenever his relationships conflict with his need to write, justifying this with statements like, "[Men] have always felt a need to be free of any ties, while women, on the other hand, are sensitive to what binds them to the earth."

What they are, in fact, is burdened with guilt and a sense of responsibility. Raymonde and Guislane are heartbroken that their daughters are so intent on self-harm, desperate to see them emerge from their miasma. They remember them as children, seizing upon occasional glimpses of innocence, intelligence and talent that lie beneath their daughters' ghostly façades, but they are at a loss to understand them. Both mothers battle their own feelings of repulsion and contradiction, wishing not only to see their daughters relieved of pain, but to be relieved of the pain of their daughters themselves.

A particular feminism is at work here, both in the characterization of the menace that exists in the world and in the construct of the family with its potential for hypocrisy, betrayal and violence.

To Anna, being in the world is to be "surrounded by a reign of male terror, omnipresent, its brutality unchallenged" – in the forms of man's inventions: the prison, the nation, the state, the army. Ironically, her mother is an agent of that very apparatus, re-educating wayward girls at the Correctional Institute where she works.

Guislane is complicit as well. "[Y]ou must change," she tells her daughter Liliane of the homosexual leanings. And, "submit, submit," Michelle seems to hear her mother saying to her: yield to authority, conform.

But submission is the way to erosion of self. When Anna looks around, she sees that "some women are stooped and bowed down while others, like Michelle, know nothing yet of the orders they must obey." Then there are the "women who say nothing and smile with complicity, like the young waitress, a pale, nameless form at the boss' side, placed there by life to serve him and his baseness."

And the pattern of submission carries on, both passed on to the next generation and repeated throughout the course of one's life. Raymonde's boyfriend Alexandre finds himself on a bus to California where he befriends a woman who is escaping an abusive relationship. We see the woman later, living with a trucker who beats her, a man she is grateful to for taking her and her children in.

It is with Liliane that the connection between the broader and domestic worlds is made most explicit: "[A]s a lesbian artist she had already known in her own family life the blind rush of discrimination which was also that of society's courts, which tore children from their mothers for a question of sexual preference, in Dallas or here, lives could be crushed, Stalin's terror was not an event from the past."

In fact, it is Liliane who is the most evolved of all the characters in the book, in large part perhaps because of this recognition. To be able to resist injustice, to remain true to self in the domestic context, may provide one with the strength to defy those who would seek to erase you in the broader world. If there is any empowering message of the kind that '80s feminism made its badge and brand, it lies here. By the end of the book, Liliane's awareness is complete: "[W]hat she knew deep down was that with her broad powerful hands she would sustain the lives of others . . ."

It is hard not to read the sentiment as autobiographical. Marie-Claire Blais, a lesbian artist partnered for decades with another lesbian artist, must know the strength that can be found through confronting discrimination.

It is otherwise hard to make any claim of autobiography. Blais portrays Anna's visions, or vertigo, as the original title suggests, with such visceral and unrelenting intensity that the reader experiences the desperately uncomfortable feeling of *being* Anna. In this sense, the novel has the quality of a *Bildungsroman*, though this novel came well into Blais' prolific career, published when she was forty-three years old.

The feeling of being Anna is largely accomplished through the distinctive style of Blais' prose – hypnotic, swirling, rife with lyric repetition and imagery. Her work reads like stream-of-consciousness as it moves across time and space and shifts constantly, mid-sentence on occasion, in its point of view.

We know now, thanks to the collections at Library and Archives Canada, that to affect this style, with its complex layering, required rewriting pages as many as ten times. The archives reveal much about the process of writing *Anna's World*. Blais did extensive research into drug use and teen suicide, evidenced by the collection of photographs and press clippings found in her collection. These inspired a series of reflections, which eventually served as the basis for the narrative. Blais' genius is evident in both the result and the process, which illustrates how profoundly her research is digested and transformed, and how skilfully she uses it to produce a novel that is both urgently relevant to its time and transcendental in its depiction of the human condition.

Camilla Gibb
April 2009

It was neither warm nor cold in Anna's heart, neither cool nor blazing, it was empty, she thought, it was quiet and pure, with untouched depths they couldn't even imagine, they being the others who let her drift like that, aimlessly, without reason, at times they smiled at her, touched her lightly with their derisory affection, then returned to themselves, to their adult preoccupations, no longer asking what she thought or felt, though it was a long time now since they'd dared ask her anything, for in their despondency perhaps they too had decided that she was utterly free, that she didn't belong to them, she could sense the will, the rigidity as well, of her independent young body against her bones, all her fiery awareness was there, stiff and contained, delicately she laid her fork on the red tablecloth, observed her mother's guests, her colleagues – psychologists, educators, therapists – whom she saw every day at the Correctional Institute where she worked, but hadn't Raymonde told Anna about some sort of meeting tonight, an emergency debate on delinquency, too many girls in the Correctional Institute, they didn't know where to put them up, yes, that was it, but Anna was still looking at her mother, still thinking, neither warm nor cold, nothing palpable, she was free and her body, free of any ties, was close to her as a straight line, not apprehensive, resting on nothing palpable or real, not even the polished wood floor under the table, she was not apprehensive at being there among them, within the walls of their house, even if they were saying in a light chatty tone, yes, we're concerned, very concerned about our young people, the future, yes, we're very concerned, if you only knew, and for them the word future was a certainty, they uttered it shamelessly, outside it was clear and cold, Alexandre said that too was a certainty for all of them. She had been on this earth a long time now, a vast expanse of uncertain, frightened moments, the long sleepless day called a lifetime, sometimes they were lulled to sleep at nightfall but she, Anna, never knew the repose that also led to certainty, it was said that life began with repose, and life was something uninhabited, uninhabitable, what's the use of inhabiting one's life, one's body, if tomorrow the future is forbidden, killed, Raymonde was her mother, but perhaps there was no reality in the bleak fact of being alive, for tomorrow that life, like so many others, would be nothing but bloody dust. Raymonde and her colleagues were talking about new books they'd read, they had already talked about the courses in criminology Raymonde was taking, now they were talking about a woman who'd been killed in the subway that morning, already nothing was left of the woman they were discussing, who would come to collect her bag, her shoes, in the final flash of her dying, Anna wondered, who would come to collect those brave objects that had been torn to shreds along with the existence they had once enclosed, an existence that was now just a phantom, a coat, a faithful little bag, shoes broken by her exhaustion, someone, Anna thought, someone would have to go there, would take up these scraps still warm with life before they disappeared from our universe, but Anna thought that Raymonde, like the others, would forget the woman, did they know their words were threadbare, words contained feelings, Raymonde would say, but Anna thought the feelings exchanged in a lifetime were threadbare as well, yet the people around her talked about nothing else, this human pack, you could hear the silence, the panting of the pack in the night, they talked about nothing else, living, being alive, like the others Anna breathed, lived, submitted to the yoke of these joyless acts, her intense grey gaze seemed to be asking her mother, what do you really want, why do you try so desperately to explain everything, to say everything, and then she remembered Philippe who in the past had taken her to his place, then taken her to Paris, a friend, a man, a drifter like Tommy, Philippe, Tommy, one morning when Raymonde got up she had found her house deserted, you thought you held someone, possessed someone, she said, but they were just phantoms you ruled, only a fleeting image remained of Philippe, the memory of a sweat-stained garment on a chair, that was a long time ago, behind her now, a sweat-stained garment on a chair in a hotel room, a moment of dizziness suddenly frozen in Anna's memory, Anna who had been lost to Raymonde for so long now, even though she had come back, silent in her presence, but the sweat stain on the piece of clothing abandoned there somewhere in space, that tiny stain proved to Anna that someone had lived, breathed, very close to her, though it was far away, in another life perhaps. The others weren't like Anna, she admired them without understanding or liking them, they seemed to glow with frantic vitality, it was hard enough for her to get up in the morning, to dress, while they, on the contrary, bustled about the metallic line of her horizon, their simple acts, running, walking, day and night, seemed to her stamped with frenzied majesty, she would have liked to say to those feet that came and went, enclosed depending on the season in a leather boot or a sandal, how she suffered at the sight of them, pierced by duty, wandering like this to their ultimate weariness, Alexandre, stroking Anna's hair, told her he would leave soon, his feet would be tired, exhausted, Anna thought, it was impossible for two people to live together nowadays, he said, so he must leave, for when Raymonde was near he couldn't write, he thought only of her, Raymonde, or of Anna, he said, we have to be curious, constantly craving things that take us outside ourselves, he told Anna the story of Alyosha, a happy vagabond who for a long time had lived for love, for human pity, nowadays Alyosha would be killed, he said, Raymonde, Alexandre, a wish unfulfilled, like so many others in her mother's life, though Raymonde had always known that Alexandre would not long remain captive to a woman, a house, and I too, Alexandre said, I'm only a glutton, sensual and curious, he'll go away, Anna thought, drift, he'll be alone then, without us, we'll be unable to touch him, to find him again, he'll be somewhere else, like me, there were dreams we dreamed in the daytime, wide awake, Anna thought, while life's relentless activity went on around us, this aggressive life never stopped, like cars driving over a bridge or people's footsteps on the street, but there were also the dreams you dreamed at night, that left you with a spectral memory, it was with our nocturnal bodies that we could finally rise up from the earth, tear through that blue of the sky we gazed at complacently during the day, but what comfort did this blue sky offer us, it didn't quench men's thirst or satisfy their hunger, at night the sky acquired a fragrant texture, like bread, and all painful sensations fell back to earth, the sky opened and we ourselves directed our minds towards knowledge, a new learning that meant grasping, at last, that indifference is life's one sublime quality, that all pain is experienced in vain, and yet, even as she stepped back from the realities that made up her everyday existence – the house, her mother, and all that dwelt in them and was close to them at any moment, the silver fork on the red tablecloth, Raymonde's cup of tea on her bedside table – suddenly she understood, once she was no longer there to suffer through each private drama and the exhausting futility that drove us, from fatigue, to live out this drama without a struggle. Anna had changed a lot since that business with drugs, Raymonde said, she was unrecognizable now, Raymonde and Anna had lost their refuge in the silence of the mountain, Anna's friends had taken over the house, but what could I do, Raymonde asked, after all, many of Anna's friends were delinquents whom Raymonde had protected, defended against the harshness of the Correctional Institute, it was her duty to give them shelter, and even Michelle, Guislaine's daughter, who had called her at two o'clock in the night before, Michelle who was still hanging around the house, whom Raymonde could never turn away, for she loved her like her own daughter, Raymonde and Guislaine had known one another for so long, Michelle had long white fingers that blossomed in the light, Anna thought, she was studying piano at the Music School but she'd never become a pianist, Anna thought, there wouldn't be time, how sad to find oneself, so young, in a police station at night, said Raymonde, what nonchalance in one so young, thought Anna, for hadn't her spirit been broken, didn't it take some imagined violation to arouse the innermost being, Anna saw herself an hour earlier, lying on her bed and freeing herself from the weight of existence one drop at a time, the injection generated a second existence in her veins which alleviated the banality of the first one, an ineffable existence, incandescent and liberated, no one dared name that hidden existence for it contained too many sorts of happiness and satisfaction, Anna thought, but suddenly – and it must be like this when you're dying – the lightning flash of time spread around you as, motionless on your bed, you descended towards the luminous void with its promise of peace, nothing was required of you, only to slip like this, drifting, like Tommy and Manon, drifting, "You think you might be pregnant?" Raymonde had asked Michelle, and then,

"I know they won't let you have contraceptives at thirteen, it's unfair, never mind all that," and Anna thought fate had already settled and decided everything, for her as well as for Michelle, there was nothing more to say, if even a speck of dust flew away it was by some stubborn whim of fate, of blind, eternal fate, and Michelle had dared to imagine that a ray of life might dwell in her, but that was the dream of an unhappy imagination, what would become of that fetus, it if existed, but it did not exist, it would never come out of its limbo, its nothingness, so many vainly hoped for lives would be snuffed out in the chaos of the approaching twenty-first century, only Raymonde believed the senescent world would be made new tomorrow, but she was mistaken, Anna thought, everything had already been settled and decided for them, there would be no future, not even in human hearts, it had already been killed, Anna wondered if her parents had sensed that on the night they conceived her, it had been in the summer, in a field perhaps, in their miraculous unawareness they had perhaps felt nothing but the avid, brutal grip of their shared youth, nature had intoxicated them with sounds, with smells, and now Anna was alone, confronting the mutilated truth of her life, Alexandre told Anna how happy he had been on the roads of Denmark, Japan, yet it was in a lonely room, with Raymonde nearby, that he had hoped to finish his book, in this room he had pondered Dostoevsky's advice to beginners: "In order to write well one must suffer, suffer greatly," he asked Anna if she had noticed the "worrylines" on his forehead, she smiled, he looked at her, thinking that despite all his affection for her he would never penetrate this taciturn, impenetrable being, it was like an image that was there but whose secrecy must remain forever closed to him, in his discomfort he talked a great deal, thereby stifling Anna's silence, "Men," he said, "have always felt a need to be free of any ties, while women, on the other hand, are sensitive to what binds them to the earth; even Alyosha Karamazov was a selfish man like me, a saint perhaps, but he had dreamed of going away, of escaping to the monastic life, when his duty was to his cruel, lascivious brothers," and suddenly Alexandre thought of a story he'd read recently, in Paris there were young tramps, often from middle-class families, who fed themselves, at night and at dawn, on rubbish they found behind restaurants, the phenomenon was spreading in the cities, how did this pack of carnivores spend its days, Alexandre told himself these young people might resemble him in some deep way, for everyone had to reflect the face of his times, they too, he thought, they can never be free, even in their degradation they can never be free of the aberration of our time, of its constraints, of the sinister events the world is reserving for them, free of the authority of those old people who will decide their future, and shouldn't Alexandre write about this, the only subject for a novelist today, he thought, the survival of the species, shouldn't he – witness of so much misfortune – go and see what was happening on the margin of life, in those zones astir with men and women of his age whom society pushed away, rejected, for they were its spectres and its shame. The Zonards of Paris resembled Alexandre, were rebels like him, they went further in their explosive anger, the humiliating toil they underwent in the zone was a display of liberty, of courage, Alexandre would write all that in his book, each one struggled in his own way, with his lost or triumphant dignity, each felt the approach of a wave of collective suicide that would submerge him; Michelle was listening to a woman's voice on the radio, a violinist describing her musical life in New York, Prague, London, "Since childhood I have been a citizen of the world," said the voice, and Michelle was listening to someone who, from the age of ten, had had no need of teachers, it's different for us,

Michelle thought, we break into apartments so we can buy hash, and she wanted to cry, not because of that but because she hadn't slept for days now, in a car with a buddy, but you slept so badly, she would tell Anna, whose breathing she heard close to her nape, I'd like to get washed here, live here, wash my hair, Anna looked at her hair, its richness irritated her, tortured her, those gleaming locks gave so little protection from the grip of cold, of death, it was placed there, on our bodies, around our faces, glossy, delicate, and sensual, as though to remind us how it would one day be disinherited, alone. She remembered a fair-haired boy who, as he walked, sent up the summer dust of poor neighbourhoods in plumes that seemed to pierce the air, the polluted air from which the sky seemed to be absent, when suddenly these two wings took flight of their own accord, like a lost ornament. Anna had turned around on her bicycle, as if to take the boy away with her and protect him, defend him, but he had disappeared, he was going to live – to live, like her – but unlike Anna he didn't know, as the sunlight played in his hair and he walked, skipped, past a brick wall, he didn't know that one day everything perfect in him, even the smooth wings of his hair in the wind, would be of no use, to anyone, and that Anna herself would no longer be there to admire them, that beautiful hair often surrounded moronic, expressionless faces. All that material, sleek or rough, as innocent as an animal's fur, would one day disappear along with us, Anna thought, even the animals we had loved and tortured, for our pleasure or our food, and we wouldn't see them again in our foolish eternity. For some time – as long as she had been seeking the meaning of it all – Anna had had a foreboding that the disastershow presented every day, on television or in the newspapers, was taking place not far away but right inside us, the slow debasement of the world had started in our bodies, in our brains, even if we refused to see it or admit it. Anna wondered, why did they make love without thinking about me? They persisted in creating so many lives and then bruising us, mistreating us, they were capable of injecting syphilis or cancer into a community of mice or rabbits, that's why those laboratory photographs resembled them, they were eaten away by syphilis, by cancer, and their descendants would be too, they were glassy-eyed, their fur was falling out, there was no barrier between them and their murders and tomorrow there would be no difference between their murders and us. Michelle was holding her head in her hands, suddenly everything seemed heavy, but she'd feel better after a bath, she wished she could tell Anna. "It would take me years to learn a Bach sonata, like that famous violinist on the radio, it's so hard when you don't know anything, when you need teachers," but she said nothing, only listened to the others talking about young people and drugs, about a new treatment centre that was opening soon, the others all seemed upset, perturbed. At that moment, Anna thought, there was in Michelle's destitution, on the haggard brow under her heavy hair, a helplessness that reminded her of the little prostitute at the Howard Johnson, that was how she thought of the girl whose illicit existence she had glimpsed one day, thinking that in the whole chain of identical restaurants that haunted the overpopulated cities, the little prostitute with her earrings, her pale face streaked with rouge, her skimpy black dress, the cough that shook her pubescent body, that hers was just one existence among all the others, Michelle was more sophisticated than the unknown girl drinking a Coke, her legs wrapped around her stool, her expert eyes surveying the males lustful with the end of day, but she knew no more about how to defend or protect herself, no more than the fair-haired boy walking along the brick wall one sweltering day, all those still-new creatures with their satin skin, their moist eyes, their unkempt hair, not knowing that they were already the prey of others who waited for them in sleazy places, that they were being initiated, without knowing it, into games of lying and promiscuity without which society could not exist. They were like stags in the forest, Anna thought, living targets, unaware of the appetite they aroused, and they too would go from one forest clearing to the next, hearts throbbing with hope, until their extinction, and yet the little prostitute had probably realized there was nothing about a man to reject, you followed him, that was all, the den of happiness, of discovery, was a narrow passage, sickening and dark, on the ground floor of a restaurant, you could learn about life there as well as anywhere, a little mescaline and you escaped, for wasn't the main thing to exist, to feel – despite cold and fatigue and the cough that had lasted all winter – something monstrous and alive quite close to you, yet who knew, Anna thought, whether that dark corner with its decrepit walls and plumbing might not represent a paradise, a place of ecstasy? You had to become like them, hide within their ranks or die in servitude to them, what was Michelle doing in this life, with her refined nature, her delicate nose, her hands working at the Bach sonata, didn't she understand that, for survival, this grace was futile and vain? Anna, who was only a few years older, would try to instil in her the notion of self-interest, of calculating perseverance, she thought, that was so indispensable for their generation's survival, but Michelle wouldn't understand; certain things fell their way quite naturally from the tables of the bourgeois, from their parents' homes and from every other social institution in which Michelle and her sisters had no rights, and why didn't Michelle take these things by force, as she should have done, or why did she associate this act of taking what was her due with the theft, the vandalism, young people were accused of? She was wrong, Anna thought, for words like theft and vandalism existed only for their false judges who were, themselves, guilty of these crimes, perhaps Michelle would learn, through our chaos, to play the Bach sonata, but she would not know how to survive, Anna thought, and this act alone was worthy of our solidarity, our love. At that moment, too, Michelle seemed to Anna like the young goat they had seen leaping with joy one Good Friday among the tables of a local Greek tavern, perhaps the owner recognized the hostility with which Anna was judging him, for she sensed, as he turned towards her, that happy, self-satisfied violence the kid would fall victim to tomorrow, which prowled about her and Michelle even as is awaited its target, not knowing how to hurt them, to tear them apart, on the pretext that it was illegal to drink at their age, but Anna felt that the violence had always been present, here or elsewhere, that this crude man was just a fleeting glimpse of a violence, infinitely more fearsome and deeply hidden, that dreamed of abolishing them all, her and the others of her species or all those who, like the young goat, symbolized this world's fragility, who sought, here or elsewhere, a refuge, a halt to man's cruelty, even if it meant being physically conquered by that mass of muscles and bestial guilelessness. Anna was looking defiantly at the man, with a challenge that should have wrung tears of rage and hatred from him, when she sensed Michelle beside her, tiny in her oversized coat, Michelle who was unaware of the evil power she would be delivered to tomorrow, for like the goat she seemed to understand nothing, she was light and graceful, the animal was Good Friday's victim, still free, playing among the tables to the crackling of an exiled music, and Anna had thought, that's Michelle's life, and mine too, almost, what is life, death, a lugubrious vigil surrounding a moment of celebration, of hope, and what was Anna's rebelliousness, "Anna's network" it was called when people talked about her and her friends, before that butcher who embodied a mafia so deeply concealed it could be neither seen nor recognized, for it was man, the city as he had made it, and everything man had touched and manipulated for dishonest ends as he ruled through the force of fear, some women were stooped and bowed down while others, like Michelle, knew nothing yet of the orders they must obey. There were also, Anna thought, women who said nothing and smiled with complicity, like the young waitress, a pale, nameless form at the boss' side, placed there by life to serve him and his baseness, and she seemed to like it that way, for she looked at Anna with a complacent smile, already rather spineless, yes, Anna thought, what was a network of teenaged drug dealers, they were in and out of the Correctional Institute, Raymonde tried to re-educate them, but why and for what, Anna thought, who were these adventurers, still prisoners of their childhood, and pursued, persecuted for minute infractions of the law? They were surrounded by a reign of male terror, omnipresent, its brutality unchallenged. It was not just the city, the world, Anna thought, that held this authority that endangered so many lives, but aside from nature, which was said to be God's creation, there was no higher authority to unleash against Michelle and her kind, Anna and those she loved, than those machines of terror that were prison, the nation, the State and, most fearful of all man's interventions, the army – each of these words that could not be spoken without fear – each of these threatened these young lives, still dormant, still stunned by the surge of their own grace, and thus Anna would tell Raymonde, her mother, that she was wrong to utter, in her presence, words she believed in like re-education, transformation, Michelle had called her from the police station at two in the morning asking for help, but Anna would tell Raymonde she had no right to utter those words, for they belonged to a State created by men who governed, they belonged to the world of law, to man, who had invented them, century after century, not understanding that they were words of terror. Then there had been that moment when Raymonde shuddered in pain as she observed her daughter's vacant gesture, placing her fork on the tablecloth she remembered the time when Anna still used to come and lie beside her when she was reading late at night, once more she felt at her side that alert presence that didn't sleep, that never seemed to rest, the rigid head in the hollow of her shoulder, and suddenly, insidiously, the air was filled with words – boredom, disgust, disenchantment with life – against which Raymonde was powerless, for these sensations were hostile and unknown to her, and yet weren't the disgust and boredom, searched out by a keen intelligence, already inscribed in the fold of Anna's mouth, on her mute brow? Then Raymonde asked anxiously, "Are you bored?" and Anna answered, smiling, "You can see that I'm thinking," and they both fell silent, the silence was even heavier today when Raymonde's gaze met Anna's grey eyes at the end of the table, Anna's ironically defiant gaze that seemed to ask, "Remember, Raymonde, when you used to steal books, how you did it to denounce the ignorance around you, and that hoard of stolen goods, meat and vegetables, how it was to feed my father and me? Why don't you remember the past?" "Your father and I were only students," Raymonde seemed to reply; "Haven't I always tried to erase any stigmas of a bohemian life that might prevent you from growing up like the others?" but suddenly the rigid little head on the pillow was accusing, denouncing, the words that poured from Anna's mouth were lucid, they recalled the existential philosophy Raymonde had once thrown herself into, the works of Sartre, Camus, books that had excited Raymonde's imagination when her daughter's remarks saddened her, above all Anna accused her mother of having lost the warlike fervour she herself had now inherited, unwittingly, for wasn't Anna's war like a war of inertia, Raymonde thought bitterly, so she thinks I'm no longer useful, but sometimes Anna's presence was more tender, like a puppy who had come to lie at Raymonde's side and be comforted, and then Anna rose suddenly, disappearing as she had come, in the khaki shirt "that she doesn't take off even to sleep," said her mother, boredom, disgust, disenchantment with life, Raymonde put her hand on Anna's brow, "I'm getting up early tomorrow, there are more problems at the Institute, you'd better go to your own room now," Anna knew that Raymonde was lying, problems at the Institute, the word her mother didn't dare to say in her presence was violence, probably a fifteen-year-old inmate had attacked her mother with a knife because she'd been refused permission to go out one Sunday, all around her Anna was breathing in the presence of that scourge, violence, the violence people refused to talk about openly, like sickness or death, but it was stirring all around her, even when she came to lie quietly beside her mother at night, and Raymonde tried with caresses to soothe this anxiety that gave them no rest. And now Michelle was there and Anna was talking softly to her, Raymonde heard only the murmur of their mingled voices, I hope she isn't telling that child about her dangerous adventure in the Caribbean, or about Philippe, she could have a negative influence on her, she had put on her glasses to see them more clearly, wasn't Anna's face softer since she'd come back to the house, or was Raymonde just imagining that her daughter could still change, no, it was like the memory of that rigid little head on the pillow, nothing was changing, Anna was living elsewhere, far away, in a transparent universe that was foreign to her. It was the Christian notion of earthly happiness, Alexandre thought, to state that each of us should find a place for his drifting body, a roof, a bed in which to stretch out his limbs, yet nothing was more unlikely – entire nations, women, men, children, lived without fire, without a roof, obsessed by hunger and its dizzying pain that numbed the spirit, they had been sentenced to movement without rest, to forced labour, like an inferior species, and they were panicking, everywhere, a living river of the forgotten swept along by the hallucinations of hunger, of despair, the fixity of their desires preceded them, hunger, hunger, and the dream that they could never attain a hearth, a home, Alexandre thought, that was how their creased flesh seemed to dissolve, they went back and forth aimlessly like layers of fog and gradually this feverish fog replaced their gestures, tempered their gaze, and once more Alexandre was projected into their midst, today freezing rain, snow, or wind marked his face, tomorrow it would be so fine that the sky would be a dazzling blue against the permanence of snow, there would be dawns when the sun took a long time appearing in the vast grey and white sky, Miami Beach, Portland, some would come to settle their stiffened limbs in luxurious armchairs in stations or airports; Alexandre smoothed his beard with his fingers, he would be beaten like an old *muzhik* before he was thirty and tomorrow Raymonde would see in him not the proud male, the fiery intelligence that talked about everything and knew nothing, but a heart purged by the bitter knowledge that everyone dreads, yes, he would go away, for her, thinking of Raymonde, Anna, of the dignity of their bonds, go out into this dark world where everyone hesitates to be joined to anyone else, impelled by fear – Alexandre would go to the utmost terrifying depths of humanity, and as he waited he dreamed he was blowing on his hands to warm them, musing beside an old man with big holes in his shoes, he dreamed of a steaming bowl of soup, of a shelter, somewhere, tonight or tomorrow, and Raymonde awakened alone, spoke to her daughter, "A class this morning, you haven't forgotten," one was never sure if Anna was really there, that echo, that silence, she had left the cage open, the birds flew freely in the kitchen, it was as if Raymonde's life were in suspense, as if she would never complete some simple act she had started, making her bed, folding a blanket, and yet none of it was real, she felt vigorous, filled with energy that she must contain, she thought, I remember, yes, I was bringing Anna home from school, did she tolerate my presence because she was too small to cross the street by herself, that was the day a woman appeared, bursting out of a narrow street, scantily dressed, her feet in glass-heeled shoes, a man had just left her, taking his things away in a truck, they were flimsy summer shoes that buckled under her, scraping the cold, hard ground, the young woman started to cry – a long cry, as if she were transfixed by pain as she rose up, as if she were going to take flight with her cry – the man, the truck, the gaping suitcases in the back, there was such a blast of violence and pain that Raymonde felt within herself the moment of rupture with life that had occurred, she bent over her daughter, oh! That unyielding face in the luminous pink of the approaching winter night, but who knew what was there beneath the childlike mask, the sealed lips, Anna had judged, sentenced the man who spoke like that, in the past she had condemned her father, it had been her first act of hatred, perhaps, or of conscious hatred, and Raymonde had thought, she can't understand, they loved one another yesterday, this morning, even just a few hours ago, and suddenly they are annihilated, who knows, perhaps at the same time they are uprooted, wrenched from the earth by the same painful, violent ascent, but perhaps each one understood, alone, how much their love had consoled or protected them from that utter annihilation each would confront some day, the portent of everything that is there, ready to explode, but less evident to a couple, Raymonde thought, the foreboding of our own death.

"Do you live here or at Anna's?" Guislaine asked her daughter. "Am I your mother, or is my friend Raymonde?" Michelle felt weighed down by the ambiguous gifts lavished on her by her parents' affection, the authority of love, and their impatience with her because they received so little in return, as Guislaine was constantly complaining, the incessant extravagance, everywhere, all year round, her life and her sister's were choked by presents they didn't deserve, yesterday it was the dancing lessons so inappropriate to her languid body, it seemed to her that even her physical makeup contained some weakness or excess inherited from them, from their nature, wasn't her spine curved, her nose too long, and now these piano lessons at the Music School, "You're walking crooked, you've been smoking with Anna, you never think about me, if I were a country doctor in the middle of nowhere we wouldn't have to deal with the influence of drugs, of homosexuality, we'd be a real family and I wouldn't have to keep telling myself, Michelle's locked herself in the bathroom to shoot up, Michelle might die and Michelle is my daughter." Michelle opened a book on her knees, Cosima, Cosima Wagner, she had lived, suffered, I'll never be able to know her, and in the meantime she desecrated the gifts of that mother love, so intense and so touching, every day, "I wear myself out telling you that I exist too," Guislaine repeated to Michelle, and always she met this block of silent complicities made up of the two sisters, Michelle shut away with her book, Liliane getting dressed to go out, "You're going to hang around with those girls in the bars again?" Guislaine asked and Michelle had just spent the night in a car with a boy, a car that didn't belong to them, before her eyes was a picture of a human body with its cells being gradually destroyed by cancer, Liliane, Michelle, they were healthy, but drugs, that contagious disease of the cities, precocious sex, all she asked was for them to be a little bit like the others, wasn't their father a young sociologist, respected in his field, and slowly, belatedly, she thought, she dreamed of the dignity of acquiring her own profession, abandoned long ago to raise the children, "I know you always think it's too late where your father and I are concerned," but Liliane and Michelle said nothing, all those lives that come and go and then suddenly disappear, thought Alexandre, a woman he had known, one of many, an elegant and pretty waitress, had asked her customers one day who owned a suede jacket that had been lying around her place for some months, and they answered that the man would not come back, he was dead, perhaps the waitress had felt some hesitant sympathy for her customer when he was drinking at night, vulgar and rowdy with his friends, but suddenly the grimy suede jacket had become a symbol of mourning repugnant to everyone who loved life, and the shameful garment was quickly thrown in the garbage, it had to disappear, no longer exist, Alexandre thought, it was as if they scarcely heard the brief silence, the exhausted silence of the drunkard going into another world, the rustling of the suede jacket in the solid green bag in which the dead were also transported, for the fabric of life was the same everywhere, tangible and real, Alexandre thought, we can no longer escape the uniformity of this wretched setting where we live.

But here I am, on this earth, thought Alexandre, to entertain myself with the thought of my own existence, contrary to what we learn in the philosophers' books, I am here to be happy, the man who was sleeping beneath the earth, the one who had been the drunkard in the suede jacket, must miss his existence, especially those hours of idle daydreams about a waitress who had been, for a moment, the judge of his passion for life; he was no longer there, even in a slovenly and lascivious form, to savour, to lament his fate, but how he must regret the memory of his sorrows among us, thought Alexandre, deep in the earth the sun no longer set, while outside the light still caressed the poor and the rich, nourishing them both with its warmth, such was the joy of the selfish and deceitful, while they lived they perpetuated the greediness of their games, forgetting that the light never touched the dead, and so the person with the suede jacket ended up hurried, debased, under that invisible dictatorship that ruled the dust, only a short time ago he had his place in the violent, anarchical kingdom above ground, and suddenly he was nothing but food for worms, down below, a gleam of awareness still dwelt in his now lifeless brain, it was a gleam of fierce desire for a life that had been lost, who knows, at that time of day when the sun was setting over the earth, Alexandre thought he desired, perhaps, a life he'd never known, that of a peaceful peasant leading his donkey at the end of a rope, in Peru or somewhere, it was hot, the peasant's skin glowed with pungent sweat as he advanced towards the setting sun, and he who had been the man with the suede jacket was thinking, even the most destitute among them is living and breathing in my place, at the end of a day's toil he can still merge like a black stain into the blaze of the sky and know that on the morrow, out in the fields, they will still need him.

The little old man with big holes in his shoes indicated with his weary eyes the metallic void of the railway station, he contemplated that thing devoid of hope which opened up before him, a sturdy boy like Alexandre couldn't understand, "You know very well that even out there, far away, it will still be winter. Young people today," he muttered, staring straight ahead, and

Alexandre thought, it's true, I didn't see Anna this morning when I left, Anna's friends, perhaps she was somewhere else, with them, the heavy way they walk at night, hugging the walls, a silent turmoil taking them far from us, mescaline, cocaine, she stayed away from it now, since she'd been back, perhaps, Michelle, Anna, the sinuous lines of their fragile faces when they drew close to read together or to chat, Michelle's curly head drooping gracefully onto Anna's shoulder, but sometimes at night their slender bodies were heavy as lead, hugging our walls, our houses, with a pounding of terrified limbs we could no longer hear, Anna, how could he leave the house without seeing Anna, the old man standing close to Alexandre seemed distracted by a woman around sixty, wearing a grey coat with a hood, like a little girl's, flanked by two policemen who were leaning towards her with an air of tolerance that resembled pity, another homeless person, the old man thought, irritated, as the policemen continued their sad and mawkish questionnaire and the fatal words were inscribed in the air: "You must know someone here, we can't let you go without a ticket, take another look in your purse." The woman asked if she could sit on the floor. "If you want," replied one of the policemen, they seemed surprised and full of anxious indulgence over the fate of this creature who had suddenly been entrusted to them, "Why yes, certainly you can sit down, but there are benches over there if you prefer," big tears rolled down the woman's cheeks and she slumped against the wall saying she could go no farther, and the old man looked indignantly at the torn woollen trousers, the tiny red rubber boots of the defenceless woman sitting there against the ticket counter, hadn't she just consented, without knowing it, to her own downfall, the old man wondered, and this misery that could no longer struggle, that acknowledged defeat, disgusted him, for her abandonment of life was marked by an indifference and pain that were linked with his own destiny, a solitary man, a homeless person, even if he was too angry to shed tears like the woman, attracting to herself tolerance, or pity, or perhaps both at once.

The birds were flying freely in the kitchen, Anna usually opened the cage when she went out in the morning, "a biology lesson," Raymonde said, but Anna was already gone, a few objects blown about by the tyranny of existence, the existence of Anna, like that of the others she met every day, lay in the corners of the bedroom, the khaki shirt, jeans worn so thin they seemed like an extension of Anna, of her skin's transparency, her muscles' elasticity, in this room where Anna had grown up, and which she had left so soon, there was a Boudin reproduction that Raymonde had put up on a wall she had once painted pink to please her daughter, Boudin's painting depicted joyous life on the beaches of Honfleur, turn-of-the-century swimmers who, though they were no longer close to us in time, turned static profiles towards the sky, all the sensuality of summer halted there, in the contentment of a serene bourgeoisie, immutably awaiting their pleasures, and why should they be blamed for loving the air, the sun, and the sea, for coming to lie beneath a perfectly blue and painless sky, their bodies greeting the joy of living today, the hope of enduring tomorrow, why reproach this chaste seascape except for depicting something we no longer were, and would never again be, an already distant paradise we had destroyed, no, Raymonde protested inwardly, no, those are Anna's ideas, we haven't destroyed anything, and she heard Anna speaking with such resigned sweetness sometimes, her voice repeating, those people repel me, their sky, their sea, under that serene and peaceful air there's nothing but cruelty and hypocrisy. "But they're people like you and me," said Raymonde. "When I took you to France you were happy, Anna, remember?" Anna had looked at her mother, unable to put into words what she saw and feared on the other side of this painting where water and light spread out in all innocence, the way nature was made, she enclosed us without seeing us, the sun's rays exhausted the man weakened by hunger when, elsewhere, they fed off green pastures that shimmered before our eyes, water, air, light, all reminded us of our lost innocence in a world where we would condemn them to exist no longer, except in paintings. Anna felt a sudden urge to leave this life, this earth where she hadn't even the freedom to choose, as her mother had done before her – no choice, perhaps, she thought, except to become, tomorrow, an involuntary witness to the genocide of her generation, was there any injustice greater than realizing that you were deprived of life even as you were given it, that this task of saving lives, which required so many hidden angles, such delicacy, was entrusted to senile brutes who held your still innocent destinies in their power? No, for Anna this corner of the wall that Raymonde had once painted pink was a theatre for events so mournful that water, air, and light, along with the haze of colours formed by the blobs of the painting, seemed distilled into the dried blood that announced the extinction of her life as well. And those birds have fouled my house again, Raymonde thought, shaking the dust from the curtains, Anna was still there, in the wake of this animal life she left behind her, the parrot, the doves, and the dog they would have to part with because she always forgot to take. him out, everything here was tied to Anna, to a perception of the world that was hers alone, to the way her thoughts drifted when she didn't go out for several days, not knowing if it was day or night, and to the smell of the animals that kept her company on her raft in this shipwrecked corner that her room had become, even though she was back now, even though she seemed to have returned, there was, all around, a headland surrounded by sea, that still isolated her from everything, Raymonde thought. "I sent you to the best schools, you and your sister, and now you spend your nights in stolen cars," said Guislaine to Michelle, who could hear right beside her the sound of fists rubbing nervously against the door, even though she was separated from her mother by a wall, she did not move, the blows came and went imperceptibly and Michelle waited for the end of this crisis that she knew so well, motionless, subjugated, Cosima Wagner, Michelle had scarcely had time to read a few pages of her book, yes, they had gone to the best schools, and now to the best colleges, Guislaine had a right to complain, to rebel, "You were preparing for your piano examinations and suddenly, well, what happened?" The voice came closer to Michelle, humbler, vanquished, it was like the voice of a psychologist, the voice Liliane despised so much when someone was talking to her sister, "Your father and I would like to understand, but how can we unless you say something," and Michelle saw once more that passage of her life composed of love and devotion to music, hadn't she passed to the other side of life, like Cosima Wagner, but without having accomplished anything yet, abruptly uprooted from what had been, yesterday, her strength, her life force – love, of which they knew nothing because all they talked about was sex; music, of which they also knew nothing, persecuting one another with hostile sounds. How would her life from now on be eroded by people and by things, submit, submit, her mother's voice seemed to repeat, because we're older than you, yes, she and Liliane had been forced to enter the shameful old tapestry that the world had become for their parents who, out of the hardness of their hearts, had imposed this agony, for they had been born in order to live like their parents, to discover the poverty of their language, you knew that when they talked about their children, under all the words and peremptory declarations, they were afraid of everything, they particularly didn't want to know who they were, how they lived, so in the future they would be impervious to everything in them that was still sensitive to pain, to failure, and Michelle suddenly thought of the woman who had come from Geneva with a visiting orchestra, who, during a pause in a Bach Mass, had started to yawn, slumped over her cello – that was an example of deterioration through time, to be playing Bach with a great orchestra and no longer feel anything – but for the woman from Geneva music was just a job, who knows, perhaps she loved the cello even though she'd been attacking it in a surly way for more than forty years, perhaps she played a minor role in this orchestra which travelled all over the world and she had started yawning, thinking only of herself, who knows, of her corpulence, which embarrassed her, or her rheumatism, for suddenly – the pressing need to earn one's living, to come home and rest, exists for everyone – perhaps the abandon on her contorted face had expressed only that anxiety to survive, to end her days comfortably and in dignity, who knows, even if Michelle hadn't noticed, if all the same there wasn't something like a soul in the fat woman draped in black who fidgeted on her straw-bottomed chair, sighting impatiently during a Bach Mass?

The little old man was still muttering when he saw Alexandre, knapsack on his back, board a bus that seemed to be taking its passengers to Hawaii but that probably wouldn't cross our own borders, thought the old man, Alexandre waved to him, then disappeared, the old man felt like a mummy in the stiff grime of winter he still bore in his clothes, which he never changed, he looked greedily at the still-full ashtrays all around him and, at the bar, the beer foam slowing dripping to the bottom of the bottles as though to torment him, hairy, bearded, and useless to society, he muttered, and the bus moved away with everything that was outside, the blue sky, the budding branches, and that exaltation of the human voice in the springtime streets – except in the heart of the old man who saw once more the woman in the hooded grey coat, who looked like a little girl, she disappeared through a secret doorway between two very polite policemen who said, "No, madame, don't be afraid," she'll never be seen again, the old man thought, Alexandre was leaving, borne away by an ardent urge for freedom, where was he going like that, he had no idea, but the houses, the streets gradually melted beneath his gaze with the density of the light, he told himself that far from here he would no longer be the same, a woman came and sat beside him, roughly pushing her two sons, Marc and Pierre, who, like their mother, had delicate faces, but unhealthy teeth that made all three look like vestiges of an earlier time, suddenly they were there, the mother with her packages, for she had just left home, like the old man she was homeless now, and her two sons, Marc and Pierre, whose expression was sensitive and gentle, Alexandre thought, observing them surreptitiously, where were they going, "To an uncle at Old Orchard, if he's still in the land of the living," said the woman, all that because of a husband, a man, Alexandre thought, a man like him perhaps, whose poverty had thrown her out on the street, this woman who came from Asbestos and refused to tell Alexandre her name, "When you're nobody you have no name at all," she added angrily, on the street with her packages, her two sons, suddenly finding herself with just what she had on her back, the woman's good flowered dress already creased, Marc and Pierre – their mended trousers gifts of cousins bigger or smaller than they, their shoes without laces gaping on their bare feet, they, their worn clothing, their crumbling packages, "There's nothing in them but my wedding dishes," said the woman, "and a few toys" – they had just felt the shudder of a life coming apart, it terrifies all the living, thought Alexandre, and he remembered as well the poor he had seen at prayer in a church in Spain, bathing the robe of the Virgin with their tears, their kisses, so much pleading, so many innocent tears were soaked up by the sumptuous robes of our saints, and here too, against Alexandre's shoulder, and he didn't know how to respond to this human affliction except by saying to the woman from Asbestos, "You'll see, it will be fine there, since you'll have nothing more to be afraid of, you can tell me your first name," the woman smiled with mistrust but her younger son took out his toys, as at the feet of the Virgin, and the saints in the churches, the need for hope was stronger than anything else, one couldn't help believing, placing one's reckless act of faith in life, that's why Marc had taken out his toys, and his mother gave a brief smile under her thick glasses, they too were going somewhere else, far away, deserted beaches, woods, the nighttime silence of cities, far away a more clement nature would bring them everything they were denied here at home.

Anna leaned her bicycle against the wall, wondering if her father had noticed her, heard her, breathless at the top of the hill, her hair falling onto her face, her red T-shirt with its powerful odour, he saw everything, heard everything, he must be breathing in her smell from afar, perhaps he had wondered, why is she coming, does she need money again, it's tiresome having to see her every six months, I only do it for her mother, or was he thinking, as he saw her kicking at her bag of books in the grass, I didn't like chemistry and biology either, she's like a part of the universe, my daughter, she is blonde like me, her bare arms will turn brown, you can see she feels good today and that makes me happy, but he said nothing as he came towards her, looking morose, he suddenly noticed that she was "dressed in rags, as usual" and told her, "Move your bicycle, it bothers the neighbours there," they were his neighbours, not Raymonde's, not Anna's, and Anna walked behind him, heading for his house, then into his backyard where there was a garden and a swimming pool that had just been installed, "That's my new swimming pool," said Anna's father, "and over there, my daughter Sylvie, who'll be two years old soon," the lime trees were puny this year, "my new little daughter," he said, the lime trees were punier than the little girl, who ate too much, Anna thought, he continued to smoke, looking morose, flicking his cigarette ashes into the red tulips and a pile of dead branches he was going to burn, he peered at the sky and occasionally leaned over towards Anna, but never to tell her that she too was part of the universe, like the house or the pool or even Sylvie, who was learning to walk and often fell, but to observe that he was wasting his money on her lessons at the Ballets Russes because she didn't go there any more, was there a serious reason for that, no, the reason was that "Anna makes a mess of everything, always, everything," he said sententiously. The good, corrosive sun made everything tremble, the air, the smoke from the blazing dead branches, her father's silhouette, suddenly unsteady, bent towards the fire, and tears came to Anna's eyes, I'm dreaming, he thought severely, she can't be crying, she's young and attractive so she weeps just to attract the attention of adults, he said, "Think of the future, what's the meaning of those tears, straighten up," perhaps he had said nothing, but it seemed to him that in this sunlight, this unsound air where everything trembled, the slightest breath of life, that Anna herself was ascending like smoke to the sky, Anna, her father whom she must call Dad or Papa, not Peter as she had in the past when he was just an out-of-work choreographer and her mother had brought him back from California, that Peter rose up in the smoke with Anna, "I'm not perfect," he said, with feigned simplicity, she thought, "but I knew – unlike some people with whom I spent my wild, extravagant youth, I knew how to be part of society, it took work and perseverance, you know, I had to fight myself for a long time," feigned simplicity, she thought, listening to him, "You'll see, without other people you can only vegetate, die, as a conscientious objector I lost my homeland and the respect of other men," Anna looked at her father through the flames, listening to him, Peter, Anna, Raymonde rose up to the sky with the smoke, her father's hopes, his freedom – a fugitive's – she saw through the flames a man who was perfect but oppressed, Sylvie babbled, laughed, "Be careful of the flowers," said Peter, "don't touch everything, you mustn't." "She can't know," said Anna, "she can't even walk yet." "If you'd learned that earlier you wouldn't be what you are today," it was just a notion that had strayed into his awareness as he gazed between fire and sky, for he hadn't expressed the notion, Anna thought, you couldn't hide anything from her, that was her one strength, you couldn't hide any lies from her. "Come for a swim this summer, in our pool, if you want, but don't bring your friends, we don't want any of that here," what did he mean, she was afraid, her father's contemptuous words fell into the fire with her lacerated soul, amid the dead branches, trampled and charred, it was for him that the honest Raymonde had learned to steal, he had to have steak every day so he could dance at night, Anna was a spoiled child, a modern child, he would have liked to reproach her for it but what good would it do, they would never be reconciled, and now Peter's hunger had been satisfied, Anna thought, and she was only the shadow of his shame, he would have preferred never to see her again. "Come here, give me a hand," he said, "you used to be able to build a fire, we've spent cold nights on the beach," and he was often sick, Anna thought, "You're going to go on with your education, as your mother wants," back then Raymonde would lay her cool hand on his burning forehead, around the fire, in the smoke of those evenings without bread or light, he would wander off alone, not wanting to be touched, they had taken him to the hospital, he had syphilis but he was still Peter, her loving father, debauched, she had shared that moment of shame and suffering with them when they were still parts of the universe, when Dad was still only Peter, not this perfect specimen who had stopped dancing because he was too heavy, and tears came to her eyes, froze there under her eyelids, while Raymonde, Peter, Anna, vanished in the smoke. "You're drifting away," he said in a tone of extreme resignation, "Why, Anna?" and she saw the fire that was going out, that would soon be only glowing coals, ash, her face, her arms were still hot from it, but she moved away from him, walked towards the cold path, towards her bicycle leaning against the wall in the sun, she, Anna, and the cold, translucent object slipped past walls, houses, drifting away, that was it, like Tommy, Manon, and the others, in jail if they didn't keep slipping away, slipping away beneath the Florida sun or elsewhere, she was light and Peter no longer inhabited her, and that was how Philippe had seen her coming towards him a few years earlier, offering him medicine he couldn't live without, she had held out the precious envelope, he had closed his trembling hands over hers, Peter too had, in the past, been able to conquer the obstacle of fear, Anna had told Philippe that she wasn't "a real pusher," the police were looking for lots of fourteen-year-old girls who slipped away to

Florida but Anna wasn't a real pusher, it was a service she liked to provide occasionally, but as a challenge, the envelope had been given to her by a boy she didn't know, in the Miami airport, like Peter in the old days, she would be unmasked, searched by customs officers perhaps, but the obstacle of fear would be overcome, she would bring Philippe a message of deliverance – the right to love, to adventure – a regular drug user didn't crush you with his protection, she would choose him, love him, as long as they didn't come and take away that right from her, the right to love, to adventure; Philippe, an architect, had drawn up plans for a city of the future even though his past and Europe's past still haunted him, "Heroin, no, you shouldn't," he told Anna, his own life, his present, were coming to an end, but life, the future and its errors – on that brow, on Anna's rigid brow, he could still see them, clear, opulent, even if, all around him, every event in the world seemed pathetic, stamped with the same exhaustion, the same weariness. Drifting away, Anna thought, Peter had known nothing of Anna's disappearances, or of her total eclipse from the world, Raymonde had never betrayed Anna's absence from the house, scorning that masculine authority which she struggled against every day, at the Correctional Institute, in Juvenile Court, she was waiting for Anna, silently, no, Peter had known nothing, thought Anna, who during that time was following the indiscernible course that tore her away from her mother, and her mother from her, San Juan, Saint Thomas, they all dreamed of travelling to the Caribbean, the hope of sunny beaches, of days at sea, during those winter months when Anna no longer was, no longer seemed to be of this world, Raymonde waited and hoped behind a window covered with perpetual snow, volcanic beaches, days at sea, suddenly one word came to her numb soul, a postcard hastily written from a port of call and, written in a silent hand, just "Anna," on the wall once painted pink the Boudin reproduction embraced Raymonde's sorrow, her isolation, and the silence enclosed with her, in the bedroom, Anna's room where her other captives went round and round, the doves, the parrot, her dog, they were all inseparable, for like Raymonde they anxiously awaited the return of the girl who filled them with a fearful, grieving love, and they came and went, in the doorway of the bedroom, around the bed, telling themselves that, yes, she might well be there, might suddenly return.

The woman from Asbestos was watching her sons severely, Marc was right, soon they'd be in the country, far away, why did the older boy look so much like his father, she disliked his pointed chin, his nervousness, she would look daggers at him, telling him to "stop squirming around like that," Marc, the younger one, still aroused her tenderness, her concern, he was humming, "I'm a motor, Mama," and guided his tiny cars and airplanes along his mother's arm, in the folds of her dress, "My good dress, it's all wrinkled," she said, but it was Pierre's ear that she grabbed and pinched in a gesture that had become automatic, mortified, Alexandre saw the boy's earlobe turn red, such a soft, tender earlobe, no, she shouldn't go at him so fiercely, the woman from Asbestos already felt some regret, "But he's tough, you know, you can't hurt him," she said to Alexandre, all that because of a man, Alexandre thought as he looked at them with pity, who knows, a lazy one, a dreamer, the troubles of the world always come to rest on innocence, Pierre's ear, his hidden tears, perhaps he secretly moaned in pain when his mother wasn't watching, we had no answer to Dostoevsky's question, no answer to that constant interrogation of our lives, how to justify God or men in the face of the tears of the innocent, we didn't even dare ask that question nowadays, so immanent had our cruelty become, so functional, so tied to the destructive mechanisms of our time, and wouldn't the coming frost kill an incalculable number of these early flowers?

With the approach of summer and warm weather everyone thought only of himself, of how long his own life would last, even the woman who came from Asbestos and her sons looked hopefully at the vast green fields where cattle came to graze, and the families who picnicked on the grass, heedless of air pollution, went no farther but got out their tables and chairs, staring wildly at the expressway, for they felt the countryside had come to meet them, two young people stopped at the border for drug infractions were moving on, escorted by policemen who handcuffed them and put them in their car, it was useless to humiliate them like that, Alexandre thought, because they weren't resisting, I'm like them and they're like me, he thought sadly, they all wear the same jeans, the same boots, they like to live among themselves or alone, in the mountains, in India or somewhere else, but above all they are looking for peace, silence, a healthy, viable existence, like Alexandre they didn't want to fight or perpetuate the war games of their ancestors, and many would end up, like these, losing the best years of their lives to the civilized torturers awaiting them everywhere, at borders, in discothèques, they were watched wherever they went, Alexandre thought, incarceration, death, were often the price of a burst of freedom; the woman who came from Asbestos held her younger son close to her, the arrest of the young people at the border added to the precariousness of her existence, how would she and her sons endure society's autocratic laws, they who must henceforth live outside those laws, and the privileges of law as well, in that zone where men and women like them must struggle, stricken forever by a destitution that set them apart from their fellow creatures? Already they must answer the customs officials' questions, pretend to be like everyone else, to be worthy, when those who judged people according to their wealth were presented with these defenceless creatures, two children with tormented smiles, so poor in their cousins' clothes, and their mother watching them with compassion, drifters, runaways, Anna thought, that was how her father referred to anyone who didn't live as he did, within the law, Anna slipped to her knees in the grass, in the past she had often come here to wait for her mother, on this university campus, Raymonde, Guislaine would no longer come to meet her, to meet Michelle, as they had when the girls played innocently under the trees, "Ghosts, they're only ghosts of what they once were," Michelle's mother would say, such a short time ago, already ghosts, but was it important to think of their opinions, here, as in her own room, Anna felt happy, exhilarated at being alone on her island, her books were scattered all around her, she enjoyed the sun's warmth on her body, the cool shade under the trees, she was here in this park, spilling her face into the grass, far from the monotony of traffic-filled streets, from the clamour of all those uniform lives that brushed past each other unaware, or flying by on her bicycle with Tommy, Manon, in Florida or elsewhere, that was all she knew, drifting away, abandoning herself to the ecstasy of the moment, hearing the beating of her heart, amazed as it grew faster against the silent earth, suddenly petrified in its warmth, its perfumes, for this moment of emotion, of vitality that was hers, and that would never come again, not in this world or the next.

"A talented girl who's studying at the Music School," said Michelle and Liliane's grandmother as she drank her tea. "More sugar or lemon, Grandma?" Guislaine asked her mother-in-law, the old lady gazed at her, her black eyes sparkling with curiosity, "They aren't here, I see, they've gone out again." Guislaine smiled at her mother-in-law without seeing her, she wasn't thinking about her but about Michelle, whom she hadn't heard come out of the bathroom, the book inspired by the life of Cosima Wagner had been forgotten along with Michelle, amid her music books, the syringe, the powder, tools of death, Guislaine thought, lowering her gaze, "I thought I'd drop by, since I was at the hairdresser's," said the old lady, her lips working, "but of course they've gone out again," Guislaine watched her mother-in-law's fluttering lips, her black eyes that sparkled with noxious curiosity, "They're never here, they're never at home," she said, my imagination is too vivid, Guislaine thought, you saw a lot of them dying of overdose, in Emergency, but you never thought of your own daughter, only of others, it was like homosexuals, sometimes you heard good things about them, sometimes bad, but she never thought about Liliane, her own daughter, there was no proof about Liliane, only doubts which seemed more and more concrete, were others to blame if Guislaine had doubts about everything, was it her children's fault, didn't her husband write brilliant articles whose quality also inspired these doubts, this uneasiness, she wondered sometimes if he was sincere, doubting everything, that was it, one could be sincere and arrogant, now the old lady was saying how much she liked "the sunny apartment, the plants in the living room," deep down she's provincial and naïve, thought Guislaine, why be annoyed with her, the authoritarian line of her nose, her chin, reminded Guislaine of her husband, the old lady's thoughts came rushing to her lips, she seemed to be pleading, silently, "Why don't you talk to me frankly about this business of sex and drugs, why do you let me remain so ignorant of life?" but she also seemed to be saying, "No, I don't want to know any more about it, since my husband died nothing interests me any more, why don't old couples die together?" What has become of my charming granddaughters in their schoolgirls' tunics, the old lady was musing, she had taken them to church when their atheistic parents still allowed it, but without God you were soon led down the path of error, of sin, there was ample proof it all ended badly, why didn't people listen, they were the Lord's lost sheep, after Mass she played cards with her friends in the neighbourhood, they could hear the little girls laughing as they played on the swing, at four o'clock she would come and bring them their snack on the lawn, "They're delightful, are they yours?" "Yes, they're mine," and suddenly she no longer had any granddaughters and Sundays were tinged with the same boredom, the friends who played cards, their chatter, which exhausted her, and the recollection of the hours that would never return, the swing was empty, silent, her friends drank orangeade on lawn chairs, no children climbed in the trees, her grey-and-white cat was a creature that, with advancing age, enjoyed only its own comfort, in summer it slept all day on its cushion in the big living room where the clock struck the hours, no, the old lady didn't understand why or how she had lost them, "My pets," she sighed, "my poor little chicks, what kind of world do we live in?" Peter had a new house, Anna thought, a new wife, one of his students, so young she seemed like Anna's sister, they had given a gold bracelet to the little girl who was learning to walk by the swimming pool, on it was engraved her name, "Sylvie," that way they wouldn't lose her, Anna thought, Peter had picked Sylvie up in his arms and Anna had thought he was holding up to the sky, in the hot and smoky

35

air, not just the bundle of pink flesh called Sylvie, but the offering of his virility, for Peter had at last become a man, with Sylvie, and the sparkling gold bracelet crowned his work with joy, with vanity, "My love, daddy's little darling," he had murmured to Sylvie's breath, to her cheeks as he held her so close to him, had he thought at the moment, Anna wondered, of the threat that hung over those cheeks, that silky hair, had he thought when he conceived Sylvie, as Anna had thought yesterday, of the army of present-day Nazis, the most skilful, the most subtle in our history, for whom that tender pink flesh would be – tonight or tomorrow, as they said themselves, in the utter inhumanity of their minds – merely strategic points in their experimental wars, had Peter thought of the arsenals of criminal ammunition prepared for these tender targets, we were now in the era of accounting, we learned from television, from radio, that millions would perish in the next ten years, the precise figures were set out in the newspapers, physicists from all over the world met and concluded that we lacked medical resources, for in the age of accounting nothing was left unsaid, disaster was admitted, not just conceived but conceivable, a collision of interests between the powerful, and the figure was exact – from 70 to 160 million dead in one country alone – soon it would be taught in school, for we must know everything so we'll be prepared for our civilization's ultimate sacrifice, and what would happen then, Anna wondered, presidents and their armies would fly over our craters of blood and ash, they would travel by helicopters, happy vacationers fleeing mass graves filled with bones and blood, far from our long, cruel agony, they would go to their sumptuous retreats with their provisions, their wives, their defence arsenals, and from there they dreamed they would continue to dominate our annihilated wills, here and there 160 million dead and, among them, the tender pink flesh of Sylvie,

Sylvie would not even have time, perhaps, to learn the language of mankind and to understand why she dwelt on earth, Anna had recognized Michelle walking towards her, down a tree-lined path, past the university buildings, her gait was evasive, dislocated, she seemed to be staring into the distance, but she was following the tree-lined path with a sort of applied attention, perhaps she was afraid of falling, Anna thought, from time to time her small white hand would touch a wall, then nothing, Anna waited for her, sitting against a tree, wondering what Michelle saw, with her blind eyes, up in the sky, what Michelle was hoping for, waiting for, whether she was coming from the subway where you met the wrong sort of people, her mother wouldn't have let her go out like this – the torn sweater, the rumpled old skirt, the winter socks in summer – she was so pale against the line of the sky, but she walked obstinately along the tree-lined path, why was everything becoming hideously blank, empty, hollow, the sun, the summer, the transparency of this summer's flame, at the same time Michelle could feel cold sweat against her bones, she was approaching, walking as on a tight-rope, she thought, a knife-edge; her hair, like the stringy yarn of her sweater and socks, everything seemed to be coming undone, separating under the white sky, on all sides horrible sounds, screams, but no, Michelle thought, you could hear nothing but the traffic in the street, the rumbling of the subway, people reading and resting heard nothing as they lay in the grass wearing shorts or bathing suits, all was silent as before, Michelle saw Anna sitting stiffly against a tree, she saw her parted lips, the whiteness of her teeth, "Come here, what's wrong?" Anna cried, she had been called, Michelle was still alive. Sitting next to Anna, Michelle suddenly felt tears welling up in her eyes, tears that didn't flow, dry tears, Anna seemed asleep, her head thrown back, these tears on her skin were irritating, painful, and no one could see them, everyone was thinking, she's not really crying, they're dry tears, they were asking her, "But why are you wasting away from one day to the next?" She didn't have the strength to answer them, she was preparing for a piano recital with some other students, before her teachers, and stinging tears were sweeping over her face. Anna seemed asleep, even in sleep you could sense her sorrow, this oppressive sorrow and the dry tears that didn't flow. But if you could leave your body for a few moments a day, Michelle thought, there was a good reason why it was called "a trip," because everyone had a duty to come back, without the return it was a brief second's dazzlement, then utter annihilation, none of what she was contemplating now would still exist, no tree, no flower would come to console her, no longer would she hear the breathing of Anna who seemed asleep, living like them is a perpetual trap, thought Anna, with no hope of success, not even a desire for success, but sometimes you can choose to come back to your body, hesitate and then choose the only familiar route, now Michelle was back in her body, it seemed convulsive, distraught, but she told Anna, "Listen, it's me, I told you I'd be back," Anna opened her eyes, yes, the desire, the tension of existence had returned to Michelle's limbs, but she was very tired, again Anna saw her cautiously walking down the path lined with flowering trees, then past the walls of the university buildings, walls that were like cathedrals, but no air entered the dark, narrow windows, these air-conditioned buildings muffled in black, "our modern-day cathedrals," Philippe had said to Anna, pointing out the stiff lines with no inscriptions, drawings, ornaments, and the black holes of the windows where you couldn't breathe, couldn't get a lungful of air. Michelle's small white hand wandered from one wall to another, in search of a place to settle, and Anna thought of the January night when, coming home from the movies with

Raymonde, her gaze had followed a child's stray hand, it was a little white hand, like Michelle's, wandering along the grey walls with their huge shadows, a drunken grandfather was taking his grandson home, or rather it was hard to know where they were going, the two of them, the drunken grandfather shaking his grandson, still so tiny, so submissive, and sniffling in the night, "Put your mitts on," he shouted, but even as he cried the child let his hand glide along the walls, the wind was so strong, the night so cold that no one was going out, but all the anguish of the world seemed to have taken refuge around those two people, Anna thought, it was all yoked to this wretched pair, a drunken grandfather and his weeping grandson, on a threatening night when suddenly nothing, not even a city, could have a soul. Michelle was calmer now, she had shut her eyes, fleeing the glare of the sun on her fragile eyelids; Peter knew nothing, Anna thought, he knew nothing of the mornings when she had awakened alone, without him, without them, in those hidden places she had conquered, headlands and inlets where he would never go, for in these cities, these villages, in Florida, Mexico, the Caribbean, there were too many drifters like Anna, dirty, obstinate, "the wreckage of another world," he said, and what was she doing, what would become of her, those jackals she liked, went out with, Tommy, Manon, others like them from different continents, one day she too would be their victim, didn't they kill each other for a crust of bread, a bit of hashish, they were their parents' shame, tourists averted their eyes in their presence, Anna woke up alone, without Peter who never spared a thought for her except to worry about the cost of the lessons she would never go to now at the Ballets Russes, the road was sandy, Anna looked at her feet flayed from walking, it seemed to her that the fiery ocean, the sun, were slipping away with her amid the filth, the stench of these places that were hers, at times a beige dog the colour of the road came to her feet to rest from the pain of its hunger, trucks, buses, passersby wrapped them in a cloud of dust and smells, from the dog with its flaccid, wrinkled skin and from Anna's body as well, from her jeans and her tattered Indian tunic, came a haze of heat as intimate as a second skin, evanescent, gradually crumbling in the exhausted air, the haze, the dog and Anna supported one another by walking to the final rays of the setting sun, stopping only to sleep, often to sleep on their feet, exhaustion would come from drinking beer with Tommy and Manon, still by the side of the sandy road, dogs at their feet, hadn't Tommy said they'd exterminated hundreds like them in Mexico, Tommy was the youngest black drifter wandering the coast, "No, mulatto," he said, a soiled headband circled his head, it was a proud head that would go and search for food in the refuse of hotels, Tommy lived like the dogs, he understood them, the American navy didn't want him, no, Peter couldn't even imagine all that, in his complacent reclusion, where all was sweetness and comfort, for he would never come to these castaways' islands like Anna, like Tommy, where wretched creatures – women, men, or beasts – walked about, creatures who had survived every form of abandonment, every manner of cruelty, "What will we do when they come back by the hundreds?" Tommy asked, laughing, "Some day troops of beige dogs will come rushing at us, in the torrid light," they would come to the hotel doorways, they would swoop into our gardens, our houses, tomorrow, what would the peaceful assassins say who were exterminating them today, what would they say when they in turn were attacked, when their skin was slashed by blows and bites, in the begging-battle in which they had always been the victors? They must have sensed by Anna's walk, under her soft tunic drenched in sweat, that she was already less human than when she lived among them, these peaceable assassins she must not resemble, she was following Tommy, Manon, the horde of stray dogs, perhaps bearing disease and germs, but going elsewhere, towards another world, where they would be protected only by the aridity of men's contempt, and if she was learning to live like Tommy and the dogs, to steal her bread as she crawled through the dust, perhaps she would no longer be guilty of their crimes, they would no longer be able to call her, as they called themselves, "kind and sensitive," they would be silent at last, for, as in the presence of Manon and the dogs, they would no longer dare express the shame, the scandal of seeing these human brothers – young, attractive, healthy – sink to the rank of beasts when, Anna thought angrily, it was among men that shame and scandal took root.

The bus spilled out its passengers by the sea; some, like Alexandre, continued on their way, with a knapsack, a greasy hat pulled down over their eyes, others, like the woman from Asbestos and her sons Marc and Pierre, stopped here in search of dwelling, work, anxiously watching the sea and the passing of time; each one looked out at the vast expanse of water, at times grey, acrid, stormy, seeking the meaning of his fate, and each felt how disproportionately alone he was, stuck here on this bit of land surrounded by a vast expanse of water and sky, the woman from Asbestos had set her packages down at her feet, far away the legs and the arms of her sons who were running in the waves were eclipsed like white spots in the dazzling light of the sun. "It's hot," said Michelle, who had taken off her sweater, her winter socks, coming closer to Anna, touching her bare foot in the grass with her fingertips, "Your hands are cold," said Anna, but Michelle's ragged sweater, her faded old skirt had regained their ugliness and their solidity, Michelle's face was very pale under her mass of curly hair but Anna thought, it's true, after all, that she's back, suddenly Michelle was no longer falling to pieces, no longer coming undone, with those secret convulsions, those cries whose desolate percussion Anna could sense to the very depths of herself, Anna had heard words that displeased her, "Anna, Anna, I trust you, you know," while Michelle's frail fingers absently touched her bare foot, hadn't Tommy told her white people's flesh was susceptible to cold, chilly, lacking firmness, made to yield? Anna withdrew her foot, shivering with disgust at white supremacy that thought itself so appealing, attractive, that had no appeal but its blithe faith in itself, you couldn't trust it or them, "What's wrong?" asked Michelle, "Are you mad at me?" Anna rolled over in the grass, turning her back, and then, motionless, looked at the sky; the words faltered on her lips but she could hear them pounding against the cage of her skull, bound to the universe, I'm no longer bound to the universe, it wasn't the effect of cocaine or heroin, it wasn't a foreign sensation but rather a condemnation that came from herself, a decision Michelle couldn't understand, assimilate, she was so young, only a few months ago she was racing down these lanes of trees, of flowers, on roller skates, skipping as she clung to her mother's arm, but Anna had known when she saw her father with Sylvie, holding her lovingly in his arms, that there was no longer any link between his kind and her own, she was set free from the universe, she was one of a kind now, why hadn't Michelle said, as her fingers grazed the flesh of Anna's foot, "They have slack flesh," undressed they are not naked but padded with their white blemishes, they have no colour, they give off no living breath, "You're the only person in the world I trust," Michelle repeated, "My sister Liliane too, but it's different with you, I can't get to know you," and Anna buried her head in the grass as she thought, too late, not bound to the universe with them, she must go far away, somewhere else, capitulate, and yet everything was still in place on her island, the sun that burned your face, the cool shade of the trees, the books scattered around you, Michelle's pale face turned towards her, a silky expectancy she would allow to escape along with everything else that had already fled. "You can come here to swim but don't bring your friends," Peter had said, and Anna recalled that day when her father, eating outside with a girlfriend, a mistress, the future mother of Sylvie perhaps, Peter had pretended not to recognize her among the others; the sight of his progeny haggling over her music, her roses, on the streets, on café terraces where respectable people came to relax, had irritated Peter, yes, he was aware he hadn't recognized Anna, Anna and her kind, aware and troubled, it was forbidden, he knew he was behaving badly and yet he had looked away from her, he had thought, I don't ever want to see her again, she and her opportunistic generation who used their own values to obscure the true ones, his own: do not kill, do not rob your neighbour, earn an honest living, these principles had become real values, they were spreading everywhere like oil on fire, immolating even their idols, they seemed innocent, selling roses, singing and dancing in the streets, like Anna and her friends, but it would have been better, for himself as well as those who were still good, if they had never been born, Anna had held out to him her bouquet of roses, one of them grazed his cheek and he lowered his eyes in shame, telling himself he wished he'd never known the embrace of this young body which held memories of a lost life, all his recollections of his youth with Raymonde, he was disloyal and he knew it, while Anna's rigid brow was advancing towards him, threatening, he wanted to tell her, through words or silence, that he would continue to repudiate her, he would never forgive her for existing, and once again he felt those arms embracing his neck, under the gentle California sun which had excited them, deceived them, and the harsh contact with the cold that had followed, his eyes were closed, his mouth silent, he had repudiated Anna and, with her, the oppression of her love, the complicity of her dead tenderness. But Anna was no longer alone, hadn't Tommy learned from his adoptive parents, whom he had telephoned in Vancouver to ask if he could come home, that he was nothing but "a pusher, a juvenile prostitute, so stay away from us," and he would listen to them, he would not go back, he would stay far away from them, from their contempt, their insane insults, it would even be a relief, he said, to feel the end of any alliance with them, he had never loved them, he could hate them freely now for hate unlike love, entailed no servility, no dependency, Anna looked, listened to him who was endowed with this power to hate, carried away by an impulse so strong and pure that he'd been brave enough to break with the race that for centuries had humiliated him and debased him, while she was bound to Peter and always would be, through the tie of wealth, for one could not break with a race that was the only one visible anywhere, the only one visibly wealthy, you might say, suddenly one was indestructibly welded to it, to each beat of its heart, this heart that rivalled other races and was so proud that it never felt shame or repentance, "Eternity will be very long," said Tommy, for they will suddenly be confronting us, those who throughout their lives had fled, deserted, and feared us, the flow of time will be eternal, steady, for an eternity of revenge, and those who flee and hide today will no longer be able to, no, it will be Tommy's turn to look them straight in the eye and tell them, "I can imprison you in an eternity of hatred, you can no longer flee, it is too late even to awaken you to tolerance, to pity, yes, eternity will be very long," said Tommy, when we are all captives confronting one another, and the unleashing of endless

hostility, the victims finally repaying the debt they owe their torturers – so long, the days, the nights, that we shall even lose the
urge to carry on our crimes, yes, for the first time we shall be
weary. Anna wondered if these thoughts occurred to Tommy as
he used a long spiked stick to snatch up the shadowy substance
of the evening meal he would share with Manon, from the
garbage cans of luxury hotels, "which you find everywhere," he
said, "even outside the cities where people are starving to death,"
yes, at dawn, when the city still seemed silent and clean, perhaps
these thoughts droned about his temples as he snatched up
bread, meat, rejected from the tables of the rich the night before, there was also the buzzing of hunger, and the clarity of the
air, of the nearby water which heightened his weakness and
despair, but even more there was the pure, powerful breath of
his hatred which seemed to come from the open sea, as if to
sweep him away, and it was as if he were dancing or snickering
with happiness, Anna thought, when perhaps he was only
thinking that he would return one day, with the stray dogs, to
these same places, to devour the men whose leftovers he was eating today. It was when she was dozing by the side of the road,
next to Tommy and Manon, that Raymonde appeared to Anna
– in the form of a familiar being who had to be Raymonde, with
whom Anna was walking, struggling against wind and cold,
Anna, Raymonde, huddled together, trying to find their way in
a city where the obscene presence of winter and cold still lin-
gered, they did not speak but their eyes sought one another,
and Anna suddenly awakened, thinking of Raymonde's icy
arm which had touched her own, under the wool coat, Raymonde was no longer there but the sensation of cold remained, Anna was shivering, she felt chilled to the bone even
if sweat stood out all over her sun-reddened face. Often, after
seeing Raymonde in a dream, Anna would send her a quick

postcard, from one of the word "Anna," nothing more than the ghost of her handwriting, of someone who was drifting but still alive, someone Raymonde could perhaps touch, embrace, from so far away, even if Anna herself thought she would never go back to the world where Raymonde and her kind lived, never again be touched or kissed by them.

Michelle had sensed Anna's imperceptible estrangement, the sudden sorrow that came between them, Anna sat up in the grass, the straight ends of her blonde hair falling onto her face, reading or pretending to read, to study, not looking at Michelle, she thinks I don't deserve her friendship, Michelle thought, looking at the straight ends of her hair, there was hostility in Anna's body quite unlike Michelle's feelings about herself, her own long, soft body, she thought, Michelle needed other people, Anna fled them, disliking the way these physical presences moved about her, they were never discreet enough, and yet she occasionally brushed the hair from her face and looked fondly at Michelle, perhaps wondering what might be happening inside her, whether she would become Cosima Wagner some day, or nobody, but if she didn't ask her any questions it must mean she didn't care about her fate, Michelle thought, you couldn't think Michelle was somebody, "my poor wreck," her mother called her at times, always sorry to speak of her daughter that way, but in moments of impatience or anger didn't she tell her daughter, "I hope you won't be a wreck all your life," at times she also said, "Concentrate on your piano exams, you know you might do well, your father and I are on your side," because of Liliane they read serious books about homosexuality, they never said Liliane might be suffering from that disease but they said it was a disease you could recover from, at least Michelle's father thought so, and told everyone, in classes, in speeches, Paul and Guislaine would wait up for Liliane, sometimes until dawn, drinking coffee, talking in a undertone about Liliane, Michelle mustn't hear these stories so she was sent to bed, "We're a very close-knit family," they said, "it never should have happened to us," and they would hold each other's hands and weep, Anna must agree with her parents that Michelle would never be Cosima Wagner, she would never have an IQ of 190 like the seventeen-year-old mathematical genius in the United States she had read about in the papers, who had taken his life, if such an illustrious boy had felt, so violently, that life wasn't fit to be lived, what would become of Michelle whose own talents were so modest and constantly thwarted, for failure was always there, hovering over her days, she wasn't young Egbert contemplating suicide, she wasn't even strong enough to consider such a love of death in connection with an adolescent, she could scarcely imagine his magnificent brain shattering in the blast of a rifle that the owner had, of his own free will, turned on himself, who knows what inspiration, what intelligence, a future Einstein perhaps, had fled that day, forever, in the spilling of that blood and that life, or had Egbert thought, no, I don't want to become like them, a future destroyer of humanity, and thus unknowingly preserved, in the secrecy of death, the innocence he had dreamed of – for himself, and for the rest of us who had lost this innocence. Anna turned the pages of her book and the silhouettes of Tommy, Manon, rushed at her in the setting sun, or emerged from the pale sky at dawn, perhaps Tommy had sold his blood in a clinic that morning, he had seemed so feeble at her side, saying nothing, observing the luxuriance of light on water, later, at night, when they were all dining sumptuously, he would say, "There's a risk they'll sell it to whites," but there were innocent children among them, three-year-olds, twelve-year-olds in hospital with their kidneys removed, their legs, they were our countless small victims, victims of our times, and the numbers grew every year, they were poisoned by the smoke from our factories, their blood was thinned by drinking water polluted by acid rain, that was what Tommy said as the three of them – Anna, Tommy, Manon – were dining around a table that night, not crouching shamefully by the side of the road or in a ravine as they often did; around the table to which they too were entitled they bit into bread and meat fiercely, they had washed in the ocean and one forgot how their fingers had been covered with stains yesterday, the yellow and orange rags of their clothing rippling over their tanned limbs, for the occasion those rags had been pinned together, yes, on the days when Tommy agreed to lose a quantity of his blood, whether to carry out some secret transaction or because he was hungry, they all seemed ennobled by a singular, dusty grace that seeped into them, Tommy said the sky had probably scattered across the earth a mass grave of its youthful dead still rebelling against humanity and its crimes, those young dead were among them, joining them for this unexpected banquet, the tourists eating at neighbouring tables must be inhaling this deadly dust for they looked on fearfully, no longer saying they're jackals, cesspool-clearers, punks, none of that was true, Tommy said, they had fallen from the sky and borrowed from it, and from the setting sun, their flamboyant colours, and now they were gathered together for a cynical but joyous ceremony, drinking wine, eating among the living, but all three, Anna, Tommy, Manon, bore with them everywhere the dust of death, which could be breathed from afar, Tommy said. Anna listened to Tommy, wondering if he was right or raving, for a long time he'd been a prostitute on the beaches of Mexico, he said, scarcely touching hard drugs, a joint now and then, in his country, his city, the police had been put on his trail, knowing he was talked about as if he had disappeared bothered him, upset him, he said, he would work the popular beaches on Sunday, slipping into the happily moving crowds that came from the city with their children, the dense sweat of workers in search of the ocean, the sky, air, the sky cast its light on everything, the city of white villas odiously planted there and the absence of the residents afraid of the joys of the poor, the sky cast its light on everything, the murmur of swimmers in the waves, and the debasement of Tommy, which no one saw or noticed in the crowd but which lent him a strange vulnerability, and suddenly he said to himself – thinking of himself, of his body drowning in salt water and light – that he'd become edible, that his edible limbs – which they could all devour to appease their hunger, their thirst – were suffering the shock, the numbness of the waves, three young boys nearby, brothers, were pushing each other around, laughing, the youngest, who seemed weaker and unable to share his brothers' exuberance, let himself be swept along by their games, at times resting motionless on his side while the others poured sand in his hair, stroked his face and neck, constantly watchful and tender, if the fetid wind of death was coming off the ocean towards the recumbent, motionless boy, his eyes already wide open on an infinity he couldn't understand, Tommy thought, the pity of his two older brothers might prevent it carrying off his young life, still apparently so healthy judging by the smooth, dark skin, the clear gaze, all that persisted, with his need to live, set against the sad, resigned smile of the boy who already felt himself to be somewhere else, but no, Tommy thought, the boy was healthy but he was sapped by one of those diseases we've inflicted on the air, the water, the sky, each cloud that passed over his head; the wind of death would come to him and destroy him while he, Tommy, continued to feel the waves numbing his living body as it became desirable, edible, for these others that he disliked. He must become like those sixteen-year-old transvestites who sometimes served him drinks in a lonely straw hut, must become opaque like them, impervious to others' gazes, as if they were playing a role that would debase them, onstage rather than in real life, unsmiling, speaking only when necessary, in their low, melodious voices, to the client who could be seen in the distance, writing or reading, often an intellectual, said Tommy, under his straw roof, between a hotel and a deserted shower, though it seemed there was no one on this stage abandoned by life, only the intense heat of the sun moving along with the waiter, and the opacity of his hard, muscular body in black trousers and a crimson shirt, a motion- less, secret body, heading for its own turmoil, free of torment, with the sensuality of the day beneath a face that betrayed no emotion, like a wooden mask on which cheeks and mouth had been painted in garish red. Tommy's precarious existence clung like a breath to the pride of his body, to the hard muscles under his brown skin, like the Mexican transvestites he must main- tain that greed for rejection which a stranger could read on his lips, just long enough to submit, between the bright firma- ment and the iridescent water almost at his feet; and it also embraced that movement and fury, air, water, waves, all this fury spread through the seething of his blood, his thoughts, some more intoxicated than others, there were thousands of drifters like him in the world but not all were born to freedom every day, like Tommy, in other people's arms; they didn't all carry the gleam of sky and water on their bodies wherever they went, as he did, suddenly becoming a work of flawless agility, a mechanism so docile and calm that he no longer felt anything, neither love nor pain, only a tireless pleasure at being in har- mony with everything around him, man or beast, in a place that was nameless to him, in an intimacy that was his own, between sky and water, his Anglo-Saxon parents – who had had such tender feelings when they came to the orphanage to take possession of his woolly head, his smile that had no doubt evoked for them, he said, the sort of exotic innocence attributed to blacks by people who have never known any – wouldn't have recognized him now, decked out in this new freedom that every day elated him, in acts contrary to everything he'd learned with them, they were no longer present to inscribe humiliation and rejection in him, but in his silent, harmonious promiscuity, living by the rhythm of the sea and sky according to the whims of men's pleasure, wasn't Tommy a god from another time, the child of another tribe, but these dreams died at night, when dark descended slowly over his body suddenly chilled by solitude, as he crumpled some greasy paper that had contained fried fish he felt once more the giddiness of hunger, and the return of the anxiety that had made him flee so far, wasn't human nature above all profoundly corrupt and fettered, as he had always sensed, even while his adoptive parents pampered him with those tender feelings, that mawkish pity that disgusted him, touching, brushing his unruly hair, crushing his pride, the pride of his race, those same fathers came from afar to satisfy their desires inside a straw hut, with adolescent transvestites who wore earrings and didn't speak their language, no, Tommy could no longer return to them and their inexorable hypocrisy, and yet it was the time when even the humblest labourer went home to his family, following his donkey at the side of the road, and Tommy thought of each of these people, dark or gleaming with sweat, walking towards his house, his field, when drifters all over the world seldom shared in the indistinct brotherhood of night that was given to everyone, because they were still wandering, miserably, if they were to survive they must not stop, he thought, and that was how Manon appeared to him one night when he was walking, with his stick, towards a pile of garbage behind a luxury hotel, the hotel was hideously white, but Manon was going down to the ocean like a carnivore, Tommy said, all black and solemn like the carnivore she resembled, and homeless, but they came from the same country, they had kissed, taken drugs all night, Manon's sharp nails in Tommy's flesh, so smooth and clean, entwined, mingling the defeats of their races, for they were, above all, drifters, and the black rags fastened with safety pins that covered Manon's shoulders, her black clothes, the high grey boots she still had from the time when she was just an ordinary student, those high boots that were her only bourgeois vestiges and gave her an imperious air despite her poverty, all that was Manon, along with the ochre colour of her skin, and her black rags and tatters like shoddy plumage on her slender shoulders, Manon told Tommy, "I'll defend you, I'll protect you," her gaze defying the night, he listened to her, in turn submissive and vindictive in the hollow of her vulture's wing for, who knows, perhaps she was as fearsome as he, certainly she was equally bereft, for she had begged, they were united by the same helplessness, each not knowing how to survive without the other, night fell slowly amid the strangled sounds of insects, of predatory animals, which had so often oppressed Tommy's soul, and suddenly Manon was there saying, "With me your nights won't be lonely any more." Close together, not daring to move in the strident night, they longed for dawn, a pile of perishable garbage awaited them in a ravine of mud and sand, Tommy thought, like that fried fish wrapped in paper that he'd sniffed and licked yesterday, thinking of his solitary fate, but Tommy was no longer there, so alone, Manon went with him to the ravine, imperious and tranquil. Anna had listened to them, watched them at length, scraps of their existence reaching her as they shared bread or drugs, slipping close to them, into their orbit, with the discreet, unobtrusive movement that mirrored her life, her life that was withdrawing from everything, her cloistered life draining itself of its substance, but like Tommy and Manon she was haunted by a single obsession, blood, the blood of her life, of their lives, that were leaving now, never to return, they were being deprived of it one drop at a time, without knowing it, while Tommy and Manon looked for food in the garbage of the world and Anna for her soul, which had lost its ardour, its substance, in the depths of her being. Strangely, Anna thought, we used to hear on television, read in papers, that those who govern us played golf, rode horseback, we saw them kiss their wives and children when they came home from a trip, we knew they were subject to headaches, like us, but we never saw any of them tell his people that he was suffering from Anna's illness, an illness that was incurable because it was a sickening of the blood, dried blood or fresh, not one of them said he was deathly sick, like Anna, that they could no longer sustain these torrents of blood beneath the armour of their government's authority and arrogance, their dictatorships, not one of them acknowledged his unspeakable horror at having wiped out part of the planet, through scarcity and famine, they could be heard talking in their language about the economy, investments, but not one of them thought about the millions of children dying before the age of five, for the black blood of the Sahel was dry and, for them, henceforth invisible, buried deep in the earth, with the black curse, and this dried-up blood which didn't flow in the sands of the Sahel, when were they sick of it like Anna? At times the murky heritage of the future touched their speeches, but only slightly, for these men didn't suffer from Anna's illness, they travelled, played golf, rode horseback, invented the disastrous legacy of the future – without a future and without men – but they were first and foremost glowingly healthy, the legacy of the future had already begun in the stigmata of cursed childhood, while they, our rulers, would be centenarians, and still not afflicted, not when riding horseback and not when playing golf, not for a single moment would they suffer from Anna's incurable illness, while she, Anna, Tommy, Manon, and all the others, inheriting the awareness their elders had placed outside their mundane concerns and thoughts, would be deathly sick in their place, thought Anna, sick with the surfeit of fresh blood or dried, which in the meantime would keep alive those rulers who played golf, rode horseback, carefree and unconcerned. The reality of blood gave Anna so little rest that it came to her even at night, in her dreams; the weather was fine, it was summer, and Michelle was sitting on a rock in the sun, holding a music score she seemed unable to decipher, Anna approached her and a torrent of bright blood gushed suddenly from her knees, as in life Michelle smiled at Anna, seemingly unaware that the blood, so red and bright, was spattering the sky of her summer, she noticed nothing but smiled at Anna, the music score in her hand, and even in her dream Anna had the foreboding that this sluice of blood was like a promise of creation that would never be fulfilled, that tomorrow the creative flame that faltered in this heart would be bruised, bleeding, often Anna awoke from this dream thinking she had cried out but the cry never crossed her lips, it was only a murmur that awakened her, and if she was asleep beside Raymonde, who used to read or study near her bed in those days, Raymonde would sometimes bend over her, peering at her face in the lamplight, saying nothing, or merely, "It's just like you to fall asleep with all your clothes on," but she would examine her features one by one in the glow of the lamp, Anna would quickly pull the blanket over her head, leaving nothing in Raymonde's fingers but a handful of blonde hair with straight ends, she would turn her back on Raymonde and on the Boudin reproduction that was there, far removed from all this devastation and fear, in its place on the wall, the corner of the wall Raymonde had once painted pink to please Anna. Even though Alexandre was living in the house at that time, Anna thought, her mother's affection, like Alexandre's and that of the pets, the parrots, the dog whose name was Sam, seemed inexhaustible, always eager and above all devoted and patient, Anna talked endlessly then about going away, in all her dreams she saw herself already on the road, unable to return, "You must wait a little longer," Alexandre said as he was taking her to school one morning, he told her the story of Alyosha and ran with her from one sidewalk to the other, as far as the schoolyard where pot was sold, according to Anna, "Tomorrow, don't forget to walk the dog," said Alexandre, didn't she love her dog, her birds, Anna listened to Alexandre, her hand nestled in his, these days she sometimes dreamed she was going far away, then coming home with her knapsack and her clothes muddy, she was on the threshold of the house but through the window she saw everything going on inside, there was a space that led from the hallway to the kitchen door, and in that sombre space she saw her mother, Alexandre, the dog, the lives of all three of them no longer unfolded along with hers, and in the distance Raymonde was saying, "I understand you've come, for a moment, but already you want to leave," and Anna picked up her travelling bag which she had set down on the stairs, slung it over her back, and without saying goodbye to her dog she went off alone into the night, a night voraciously thick and dense, like a jungle, and this was a departure, she thought, with no return. Anna looked at her bicycle with its wheels gleaming in the sun, wheels that seemed translucent in the light of day but at night sawed at the silence with a rustling as discreet as the appearance of an insect, it seemed imbued with hope and the possibility of escape; Anna's hope, her escape and Tommy's too, sprang out of a nocturnal road, on a bicycle with silvery glints, stolen or acquired in a deal with some California pushers, the bicycle transformed Tommy as if, with it, he had been granted a reprieve, to live freely as a drifter in the real world, agile as a bird heading for a better world from which men would be banished, and suddenly the boy who had been chased away from restaurant doors, tattered and sad, had become this prince whose head touched the clouds, he told Anna, as he greeted her in the night, beneath the black night sky suddenly stripped of all the hostility and cruelty Tommy had been subjected to all day, Tommy was moving now, radiant and free like the ephemeral winged object that carried him so high, so far, and for a few hours he was rich, the bicycle with the silvery glints and himself in his dark blue satin jacket with a tiger printed on the back, they broke the silence of the night with their festive chiming, seeing Tommy burst out of the confines of a night road with his new bicycle, a tiger with golden claws charging from the back of his jacket, Anna thought it was as if this Tommy – filled with cheerful satisfaction, his teeth gleaming white in the night – was suddenly quite ignorant of that other Tommy, the one who had known utter abjection and whose ghost still haunted the stinking dens behind hotels, with the rats and all those human or animal ghosts that haunt the survival zone people never talk about, Anna thought. They would sit down at the table later and drink champagne, Tommy and Manon, leaving Anna to that sliding away, that silent drifting she experienced in their company, asking nothing of her, talking between themselves of the strangeness of this expedition they were living through, so secret, so mysterious, Anna still understood only scraps of it, tonight they would sleep in a clean bed with cool sheets, not on the roof of a bus, Tommy said, as he tore from his head the orange turban soiled with all the filth of the day, which he had forgotten to remove even as he dressed in his satin, for a night Tommy's orange turban, like his spiked stick and their food, was kept in Manon's huge leather bag, resembling a schoolgirl's bag, to which she was harnessed day and night in the service of the neutral, faceless Necessity that governed all their deeds, under the weight of her bag Manon's gait seemed eroded, bowed down, even if she still looked imperious, Anna thought, perhaps they were living this life that they called an expedition not as an adventure at the limits of disgust, of degradation, as they appeared to others, Anna thought, but as she herself saw them living, with a sort of richness, of savour, even if nothing would ever have savour for them again, for it was the odour of blood spilled or lost that dominated their thoughts, like Anna's, but the champagne bubbling in their parched throats overwhelmed them with a feeling of sacred plenitude that the others despised, Anna thought, for they had lost the capacity to savour, to enjoy, so weary were they of life's acquisitions. What exactly was this strangeness of their expedition, with its links to the anguish of survival, Anna wondered, was it that image veiled in shadow she had discerned one night, the night the Californian pushers arrived, when she was drinking a beer alone on the terrace of a café and the silhouettes of Tommy, Manon, appeared in the distance, suddenly standing out against a yellowing brick wall, these silhouettes going to meet others emerging from an old car, old felt hats on their heads – that group of silhouettes, lofty or squat, that had recognized one another, listened to one another, arguing, gesticulating against a brick wall lit by the yellow light from car headlights – that group composed, around a drug deal, an assemblage of intense details that should be called a life, or a moment of life between Tommy and Manon, Anna thought, for all the time these shadows were silently linked upon the wall, the anxiety of life was there, in the hearts that were beating faster, in the gazes that were keeping watch in a sort of trance, for they all knew the police patrolled these main streets every night, Tommy said, but the dangers themselves were part of the adventure film or story that Tommy and Manon were living, in which the imagination's anarchy triumphed for a moment over society's empty values, Anna thought. Was the strangeness of their expedition also the pity they felt at the sight of certain faces marked by the same needs, a woman in an airport trying hard to read her newspaper, hands trembling, attracting their gazes, for beneath the transparent deterioration of the face, beneath the mauve shadows that ringed her eyes and the nervous quivering of her nostrils, they recognized the face and transparency that would be theirs tomorrow, when others would see through them as they saw through the young woman, as if the white skin of her face, the mauve circles around her eyes, were merely a glass beneath which the face Tommy and Manon could see today, the eyes a liquid blue, the lips pale and quivering around a cigarette the woman didn't take the trouble to remove from her mouth or extinguish, as if this face had already started to melt, to disappear, absorbed by the nothingness that Tommy and Manon were still eluding every day, with the sun, the heat, and those chance illuminations that accompanied their lives. When night fell over a group of drifters by the oceanside, Tommy, Manon, and Anna slipped in among them on the wharfs, in the twilight softness that hid "the enemy's presence" so well, Tommy said, "under the pink folds of the sky," for the patrols were still there, he thought, ready to rise up against you, but in the trembling of evening and brotherhood the drifters forgot everything else, they shared their sandwiches with the pelicans, they were jugglers or comedians, forgetting that between sky and water they were constantly being watched, pursued, and Anna thought of Peter, how would he have judged her in this procession where she didn't even hold her own with the others who were watching the setting sun, the turmoil of boats on the waves in the distance, Tommy and Manon were drinking vodka, waiting for the disdainful pelicans to vomit their fishy dinner onto the wharfs, how would Peter have judged Anna sitting alone, apart from the others, her folded arms resting on her knees as she stared into the void, that was it, she thought, she hadn't washed for a week, she couldn't untangle her hair, she thought she might as well cut it now, or do nothing, the void, it was ironic to know she was there, in a sense nowhere, suddenly isolated from Tommy and Manon, from the setting sun, the jugglers, the comedians, and to think that Peter could see her like this, in this inert posture she could no longer change or modify, or imagine her, and finally think, there's the proof that she is no longer bound to the universe, Anna is finally dead. In front of her was another girl, fifteen years old perhaps, who had in her bicycle basket the necessary gear for the journey she had undertaken, on the wharfs, on the roads, while she, Anna, felt herself held back, suspended, scarcely travelling at all; in the basket, aside from drugs, was the girl's sparse laundry from earlier weeks, still drying, along with a bath towel that seemed to be used for everything, even a sheet and a tent, for Anna had noticed before that the girl often camped out in the street, the basket contained a box of cereal she had just opened to eat, and Anna observed her face, wondering if she too had that degenerate look, and if Peter would have spotted it behind the outward appearance of this girl, in her pink cotton dress with nothing under it but the dust of the roads and a curious sort of disclaiming of her whole being, that she had chosen the irony of knowing all that made her feel sad and drained, while Tommy,

Manon, were playing at pouring vodka in their hair, saying they had "found this bottle in a gypsy's caravan," there were fire-eaters down there, what was Anna doing sitting all alone while everyone else thought only of enjoying themselves, Tommy, Manon, they dragged her with them towards this twilight softness, didn't she see the pink clouds, the boats, two boys dressed as ballerinas were dancing against the sky, they seemed so pale and anaemic under their chalky makeup, stretching long necks beneath their shaved heads, the monstrous force of the ocean rumbling behind them, that you'd expect them to stagger, Anna thought, to sway on the horizon, their tutus frayed like the pink and blue ribbons that decorated the archway of their theatre, they seemed to be dancing in slow motion, in an ecstatic, silent gravity that troubled Anna, for the slowness of their movements overwhelmed her when she thought of the journey she wished to go on, and suddenly she felt herself immobilized and drained of strength, sitting on a wharf or by the side of the road, staring vacantly, the night wind shook the two posts and the torn curtain through which you could see the entire sky, Tommy said, and beyond the sky, seas, distant lands, perhaps still virgin, the night travelled across this fragile scene, with the drowsy dancers moving so slowly, lifting first one arm, then the other, turning their bared heads to the sky with bitter smiles, so that one might wonder, Anna thought, if the silent music slowly muffling their motions, their steps, was that of a heart stopping. Anna looked at her bicycle, its wheels glittering in the sun, drifting, drifting away as Peter had said to her, taking Sylvie in his arms, Sylvie whom he plunged naked into the swimming pool and who was afraid, "But I'm here," he said, it was Peter, her father, familiar tamer of small children who brought comfort, calm, she had known this man in the past, but Sylvie was too weak to bite, to rebel, she was trembling with cold and fear, she followed the hand that guided her, her gold bracelet sparkling in the sun, Daddy's little darling, Peter said, bending down to plant a kiss on the forehead of this ball of pink flesh, naked and defenceless, whose name was Sylvie, in the hot, smoky air Peter had taken off his shirt, Anna saw his muscular back in the sun, a proud back, arrogant, she thought, and Peter felt Anna's gaze on his back, she must be looking at him with hatred, with contempt, he thought, he would have liked to turn to her and cry out harshly, "Why have you come back, what are you doing, what are you doing here in my life?" but he said nothing, Sylvie's little feet were playing in the water, of course he would see Anna once every six months, but she disturbed him greatly, he felt Anna's gaze penetrating his tremulous soul, mute with terror, this unhealthy awareness he had had before of the failure of his life, did she sense it? Drifter, she seemed to say, don't you remember that my mother took you in, cared for you, he turned towards Anna, who seemed not to see him, for her eyes were on the fire that was going out, perhaps Anna knew that when he was a conscientious objector, young people like him were killing in his stead, bombarding towns and villages with napalm, killing, killing without remorse, sometimes with elation, killing from close up or far away, from their helicopters, elated, yes, not only by the frenzy of LSD or other drugs, but by the haze of blood that rose from the devastated earth, if they continued to kill, then it was because they had known this guilty elation, even once, Peter thought, but no, Anna only thought of herself, why should she consider the events of the world, she didn't live in a male universe, she was a selfish person, dissolute perhaps, didn't her distracted behaviour, her fixed stare suggest someone on drugs, he lifted Sylvie in his arms, her innocent, silky life, all his, still, he wrapped her in his shirt to warm her up, "It's warm, you shouldn't be cold now," he said, and Anna had stopped looking

at him, he no longer felt the weight of that accusing, denuncia-
tory gaze, she was going towards her bicycle at the end of the
lane of limetrees, all he could see was the red blot of her T-shirt,
she was about to ride straight down the hill, her rigid profile was
already closed to any surge of weakness, of false love that he
might have wanted to express, she was like her mother, he
thought angrily, she understood everything, "You can come
swimming whenever you want," he shouted into the air, but
Anna was no longer there, the animal odour of her T-shirt still
got in his way, they had the same blood, perhaps the same
odours too, but he wouldn't see her again for some time, and
Sylvie was holding out her arms to him, "I love you," she said
fervently, "I love you," but she was asking for the banana he'd
forgotten to prepare for her snack, he stroked the child's wet
hair and said gently, "Don't be afraid, I haven't forgotten you."
She, Anna, and that cold, translucent thing, her bicycle, were
gliding past the university buildings, down the tree-lined road,
and Michelle was there, already far behind Anna, wondering
why she was being left this way, without a word, she had
touched Anna's bare foot in the grass, telling her, "I trust you,
you're the only person I trust in the world, and my sister Liliane
of course," and suddenly Anna was on her bicycle, moving
silently down the tree-lined road, going so far away that
Michelle might not see her for days, months, you couldn't tell
with Anna, she hadn't said anything, she stopped for a moment
to look at Michelle from a distance, now she was making some
indecipherable gesture, but Michelle sat motionless against the
wall, her books under her arm, not daring to move, remember-
ing how her mother would have disliked seeing her with Anna
in the park this afternoon when she was supposed to be preparing for exams, when her father asked her every night, "Are you
making progress?" It was the day her grandmother came to the

house on her way home from the hairdresser, they would be talking about her again, about her case, "a case for a psychiatrist," her father would say, perhaps one of his colleagues, and once again everything became hideously blank and filled with echoes, without Anna, where had she gone, why had she left so abruptly, why didn't Michelle have a lover, or several, as Anna had done so early, Philippe or another, not a boy, a mature man, why did she stubbornly remain chaste, and love music, when her father, her mother – always absorbed in their work, their studies which they spun out – never listened to a record, when everywhere in the house you heard the silence of studying, and the discordant sound of Guislaine's voice heaping insults on Liliane because she'd come home late or not at all, Michelle sat motionless against the wall confronting this action to be performed, this gaping action that was her preparation for life more than life itself, suddenly she understood that her own life had not yet happened, that everyone was trying to fashion her, remake her in their own image, when it wasn't certain, she thought, that she had really come out of the void.

Anna glided past walls, past houses, she would shut herself up in her room and never come out, perhaps in her mute, cloistered existence these tormenting thoughts would gradually be obliterated and the flood would ebb from her, or must she live like Tommy and Manon, always on the lookout, they watched constantly, their eyes, their hands never knew a moment's rest, a picture on a wall, a tip left on a restaurant table, wherever they went this power to assimilate was awakened, along with their vigilant eyes, their skilful hands, and they couldn't meet anyone, even the most destitute of the drifters who had come from Arizona on foot, Anna thought, without considering robbing him of, who knows, a bit of rope, a knife that might be useful, they never stopped watching, evaluating, at the mercy of this unacknowledged passion, ritual and obsessive, the passion to devour the other alive, is this the way we must live, Anna wondered, or should we succumb to a comatose peace in which the other was not eaten alive, but killed indirectly, in a mute, cloistered existence made up of inertia, in which all that was human and hence the cause of suffering would be overshadowed by memory, Anna glided past walls, past houses, thinking of Michelle, of her delicate face furrowed in anguish, must she reject the supplication on that face when just one smile, one word, would have been enough to light it up, as Peter said, she thought only of herself, hadn't he talked to Anna about her cold expression, her intransigence that reminded him of Raymonde's, while Sylvie, who had nonetheless been conceived in the same revolt, the same helplessness, represented to him love without harshness, pride in offspring that had not yet turned against him to accuse him, condemn him. What would become of Tommy and Manon on the road, constantly on the lookout, mesmerized by fear, weren't they afraid of being caught, captured, wouldn't they rot in jail in one of those insular towns you never escaped, what relative, what friend would have defended them, Anna herself had lost track of them shortly after the Californian pushers arrived, at that turn in a nighttime road where Tommy sat smiling on his bicycle, in his satin jacket, where Anna herself had had a foreboding that this vision of happiness, of Tommy, might conceal some betrayal of fate that was not so easily deceived, perhaps bad luck was waiting for Tommy at a turn in this same road where he had greeted her in the night shouting, "Good night, Anna" – or were Manon's sharp nails still kneading the flesh of his back while they warmed each other on the roof of a bus, or on an isolated beach close to the scorched vegetation where the reptiles frightened them so, or were they gliding along, towards what solitary destinies, with that knowledge they had acquired the hard way, assimilating all that was alive, had they moved on to crime without even knowing it, Tommy never talked about killing but his eyes seemed to glow with cold calculation when he spoke of defending himself, Anna was afraid to ask him if this need to defend himself hadn't sometimes pushed him to perform the act that, for some people, had become automatic, the act they no longer suppressed, that flowed from itself, without constraint or remorse, and that consisted of violently breaking off another's life, Anna didn't dare ask Tommy if he'd had to defend himself to that point for she already knew he was prepared to perform that act, if he hadn't done so already, to die, sooner or later, to kill or be killed, the cold calculation reflected in his eyes seemed to be saying for him what he dared not admit, you must be able to defend yourself unto death, your own or someone else's, the act of killing flowed spontaneously, nothing was more natural, killing was like breathing, like life.

Anna glided down the tree-lined road, Peter no longer saw her, he had taken Sylvie in his arms, was gently stroking her forehead, her hair, reflecting on the young people of his generation who had killed, from near or far, what would Peter himself have thought if, on such a beautiful day, he had been forced to submit to that bloody invasion here, around his house, in this place where he was so much at peace with his daughter, if those persecutors of innocence descended from the sky in their helicopters, destroying houses, shooting down schoolchildren as they ran, what would he have thought if he'd suddenly seen incorruptible life, his own or Sylvie's, stained with blood, those soldiers had had a view of the villages and hamlets they were going to burn, they had observed all the details with a treacherous, calculating eye, they had detected a schoolboy falling as if in slow motion, an old woman crying out beneath her blazing roof, but in their intoxication they had continued their massacre, laughing and bantering among themselves, and it was in that world that Sylvie would live tomorrow, Peter thought, under a sky armed with every sort of rage, of revenge, what would Peter say tomorrow, to the blue ethereal sky that seemed to be directing Sylvie's first steps today, when they came to snatch away what was for him, at that moment, his happiness, his reason for living, for he wasn't dreaming, these persecutors of innocence were always on the loose, you couldn't see them but they were everywhere, mowing down lives, shooting down schoolchildren as they ran, burning down villages, hamlets, those same soldiers would return with different faces, they were around, there was no talk of putting them away, in jail, for they were just like other men, leading drab lives with their wives and children, far from the scenes of their crimes. Anna glided past walls, past houses and meanwhile, she thought, Tommy's tireless silhouette was prowling, circling above a still smoking scene of rubbish, at dawn, at sunset, in the silence of sleeping cities, of deserted beaches, but didn't the world and freedom belong to Tommy and the swarm of shadows that lived with him, in the zone, more than to Peter who had forgotten their sinister realities, fastening onto Sylvie's wrist the gold bracelet that, tomorrow, would hold her captive to his illusions, his conquest of the world from above, when, Anna thought, the knell of terror had already sounded in this world, when the pieces of the framework that was Peter's universe, this world above where Sylvie was taking her first steps, were being eaten away from below by the hunger of carnivores like Tommy, Manon, and their fellows who were coming to conquer the world and its splendours from below, as avid and conscientious in their destruction of that framework as when they were gnawing at scraps, repulsive fragments, for their daily survival until the framework crumbled, did Peter know all that, Anna wondered, while he was saying to Anna, "Here's my new little girl, my new house, my new swimming pool," did he know that soon no boundary would separate the one who was hungry from the one who would be devoured, that the jackals he imagined far away were near at hand, so near that what he feared most about Anna was her membership in that race which might one day threaten to destroy them, him, Sylvie, and all his fragile happiness? He knew it, yes, thought Anna, because he was already crying out, "I don't want you here in my house, in my pool, around my wife and child," already he was afraid, Anna thought, and he was trying to keep the integrity of his world intact by turning Anna away, not knowing that this world was already disintegrating under the shock of all the subterranean teeth grinding it away, and as for his freedom, hadn't Peter already corrupted it with his spacious house with the double-bolted doors and the artificial turf that led to the swimming pool, "thieves" were everywhere, he said, waiting for you in elevators at night, stripping you of your money in broad daylight or in the subway, and Anna listened to her father's voice trembling with fear, to the inflection that seemed to say, "There are many thieves and you're one of them," he had betrayed the freedom of the oppressed, of the fugitive he had been yesterday, he was renouncing that freedom with his feeling of disgust, of recoil which he experienced when he saw Anna, in the inflection of his voice that seemed to say, "You're one of them and I despise you and fear you." In this other world of the zone, where Tommy, Manon, were still fighting over the ruins, wasn't the drifter's freedom his last attempt to

67

put down roots in the human adventure, Anna wondered, Tommy, Manon were slipping, nameless, towards the depths of an adventure only they could tolerate for, however abject this adventure, was it not bound to the appeasement of their bodies' needs, they were slipping nameless, but it should have been said of them, Anna thought, that they were vivisectors of humanity, whose entrails they would lift up to us, but in their slippery descent towards our viscera, weren't they plunging at the same time towards those thousands of others without names, those lives whose pulses were so weak we could no longer hear them, for we didn't care about hearing or seeing what was taking place so far from us, and yet so close to our field of vision, in this zone where they were contemplating, with pity, from close up, a decline, a misery we dared not look at even from afar.

The freedom of the drifter, Anna thought, was also the feeling of wandering in a strange land, a strange house, at dawn, at sunset, Tommy, Manon, emerging from the humus of the city as if to be reborn from it side by side in their rags, so bright and many-coloured, resembling the proud Indians who prayed in the churches. Tommy and Manon didn't pray, they too were products of a violent civilization, they would say, through their acts of rebellion they made amends for the humble incantation of the poor who came down from the mountain, they did not pray, they would have liked to massacre the creation of that absent God, guilty of every crime, but when the beauties of the universe collapsed under the hand of man they, like the Indians, felt nostalgic for a lost world that would no longer be governed by the pure laws of blood, of tradition, like the Indians they were nothing now but human particles in the air, in danger of disappearing tomorrow, they too were the final debris of a world, but they were far from the churches, Tommy and Manon yielded to the usual inertia of the afternoon sun, they were suddenly without strength in the torrid light, like Anna they no longer knew if that feeling they'd had in the cool places where they rested, the bewitching sensation of their own vitality, their rebellion, was still real, nothing seemed to sustain them now except the hope of drifting even farther, of taking life by surprise rather than submitting to the servility of prayer, dragging their feet over the hot pavement while they walked, breathless, past the low walls painted garish yellow or sometimes washed a very pale blue, behind which mute lives were suspended, inert, as they themselves were, the isolated sound of a spoon scraping the bottom of a bowl, or the squeak of a wheel as a car stopped outside a store that sold children's coffins, the appearance through an iron fence of the livid face of an old man having his hair cut by a white-smocked barber – all these scenes seemed to them charged with the same annihilation, the same inorganic torpor, as though everything they touched, everything they carried in Manon's bag for their subsistence, like everything they saw around them, was suddenly permeated with the same perishable substance, doomed to rot. Anna had left Peter, she was riding down the hill without turning back to him, as he held Sylvie in his arms, she would not see him again, perhaps, he was cooling Sylvie's forehead, her neck, with a handful of water from the swimming pool, but he continued to stare at Anna's red T-shirt, watching her in the distance, what would become of her, where was she heading, they had been happy in California when she was very small; droplets of water stood out on Sylvie's forehead, on her round cheeks, Anna was riding down the hill so fast that she was soon out of sight, "It's time for something to eat," he told Sylvie, carefully setting her down in the grass, such an agreeable weight, submissive and peaceful,

Anna was moving away, thinking of her feet trailing over the hot pavement, of the feet of Tommy, Manon, of feet so often bare, red or sore, sometimes at night they would stop at the side of a swimming pool the tourists had deserted, wishing they could sink languidly into sleep in the coolness, but they must remain on the lookout, nerves taut under their skin, waiting for dawn, the day and its trials under the strong sun, a swallow, alone or swept along in its sisters' whirlwind, flew past their eyes, so close it seemed to brush against the frail surface of their eyelids, before going to drink from the swimming pool, Tommy, who seemed to be dozing in a straw chair, started, laughing, touched by nature's innocence, perhaps, Anna thought, coming to tease him or gently poke fun at him in his sleep. Tommy's hand opened in the air as if to catch the swallow and, with it, the vision it represented of a fleeting liberty, his hand was unwieldy but graceful, Anna thought, hadn't Tommy fractured his left hand the previous night when they were trying to jump over the wall of a villa, you could see its orange trees radiant in the evening light on the other side, Manon had stretched Tommy's fingers out over pieces of wood, Tommy had gritted his teeth without complaining while Manon wrapped his hand in a bandage that looked like a dirty handkerchief, telling him that in a few days it would be healed, later, when she saw Tommy's hand blossoming in the air to follow the flight of a bird, Anna had thought of that exchange of caresses, of tender concern, between Tommy and Manon, she was outside it yet it protected her, indirectly, from the hostility she felt towards herself, wasn't it that night, as the swallows whirled, that Tommy suddenly started talking about when he was living alone, travelling the dusty nighttime roads on the trail of strangers and wanting to comprehend their fate, a young worker going home to his father after a long absence and the old father, half asleep or drunk, hesitating to open the door to him as he stood on the sidewalk, humbly waiting, eyes lowered on his bundle of belongings while his father peered at him from behind the shutters, who was this stranger, where did he come from, the son repeated, "It's me, Dad," but the father didn't seem to hear him, then he finally greeted his boy with a mutter and Tommy thought, this good son is wasting his life in his work, his father has sold him like a slave, no one here condemns the slavery of the children who erect new pyramids for the rich, yet this same boy could know the freedom of the drifter, an unrewarding freedom but one without compromise, and Tommy's heart sank at the thought of the young slave submitting all day long to these corrupt masters – such a mercenary attitude – haunted by the material possessions he could never attain, they would manipulate the nobility of his race, the simplicity of his hopes, it would have been better for him, Tommy thought, if he'd been just a drifter, a stray dog, but in the soul of the poor man the stray dog, the drifter, stirred up only hateful wrath, the drifter, like the stray dog, Tommy said, could die torn to pieces beneath the wheels of a van, of a tourist bus driving through the night, vacationers who left their hotels only in the mild and perfumed night, in these streets that had reeked of human degeneration during the day they now felt nothing, as if their sense of smell had been anesthetised, insensitive to their own perfumes, amid the pain of beasts or drifters throwing themselves, dazzled, blinded by headlights, against cars, vans, in that state of reckless fever that was for the drifters a drug-induced stupor, and for the stray dog the exhaustion of hunger, these civilized men and women who went out only at night felt nothing at the sight of so much evil, yesterday they had felt waves of goodwill, of pity for the animals and children everywhere who embodied endless misery, but now suddenly, they felt nothing, they had willingly suspended their sensitivity to pain and, with their souls and hearts anesthetised, they were astonished that they no longer felt anything when the van tearing through the night to take them back to their hotel crushed beneath its wheels a dog, a drifter, the drifter was sent to hospital but they just drove on over the stray dog, Tommy said, lacerating all its muscles, its bones, the hearts and souls of those who took part in these crimes, without committing them, were voluntarily mute with terror, for everyone should feel responsible for whatever occurred around him, the van was tearing through the night, it drove right over the stray dog, and Tommy, who had been forgotten, left behind at the side of the road, and who was suddenly trembling all over, for it was as if his body were already so worn out that it could no longer support him, as if he were going to die in this stupor, his eyes turned to those who could no longer see him, his arms waving limply in the air, Tommy thought, the dog that was run over is me, they lacerated his muscles, his bones, they tortured him, slowly, carefully, "juvenile prostitute, runaway children," the voice of his adoptive parents covered his own cries, all the anguish he embodied at that moment, in his wildness, the torture of his own defenceless animality, he could hear the howl of this anguish in the night while his strength, the body he no longer controlled, its skin and fibres ripped away, seemed to him to be slipping into a muddy hole, Tommy rubbed his brow, defaced by cries, in the sand, the murmurs of madness were sinking into the mire with him and would put him to sleep in the end, but that time was far off, Manon stayed by Tommy's side, his hand opened in the air as though to touch the swallow, the day before they had seen orange trees radiant in the evening light, and Anna looked at Tommy, Manon, wondering how many more times they would be killed, all three of them, perhaps they were dreaming, they would never be free, on the roads

or in jail but never free of all the crimes they had fled, and suddenly they were together, waiting for daybreak and deliverance,
Anna thought, yes, that was it, deliverance from this life that
was exhausting itself within them, within their young bodies.

Michelle was walking along the street, her books under her arm,
Anna had disappeared in the distance, all that could be seen was
the red stain of her T-shirt, the wheels of her bicycle no longer
glittered in the sun, once again everything was hideously blank
and echoing, people jostled you as they passed, you didn't know
who they were, only that they were swarming around you in a
great tumult against a white surface that must be the sky, Anna
had just disappeared into their midst, her blonde head drifting
above the anonymous crowd, she was so tall and proud on her
bicycle, as tall as the trees perhaps, from close up you could have
heard her breathing, almost nothing in the summer breeze,
Michelle thought, it was Anna, Anna alone to whom Michelle
had just said, "I trust you," as she touched her bare foot in the
grass, even if Anna, loathing confidences perhaps, hadn't listened to her, if Michelle were to go home now, in the depths of
the pain she was feeling, where was the house, there was nothing but the blank and hostile sky above her solitary black foot-
prints, but the words came back to embrace her miserably, "You
have a house, a father, a mother, you know that very well, why
do you pretend to forget?" If Michelle went home her grandmother would kiss her, saying, "My pet, you must know we
don't want to lose you," her mother would ask, "Why do you
talk to her when she's in this state?" or else none of this would
be true, her grandmother, still smelling of her visit to the hairdresser, her grandmother whom, like the rest of them, she was
forbidden to love any more, would tell her, "I prayed for you at

Mass on Sunday," her mother would tell her, "I want to talk to you alone, let's go to a restaurant for dinner," and suddenly her mother's eyes would be filled with tears, shocking, genuine tears that had to be borne, the courageous tears, the well-intentioned tears of Guislaine, her mother, her kind, sensual mother, whom Michelle still covered with kisses and caresses, even if her father was constantly reminding her that she was too big now for such "emotional outbursts," Michelle and her mother would eat out, "You can talk to me now, we're alone," her mother would tell her, and Michelle would say nothing – with her dishevelled hair, her sweater and winter socks though it was summer – they would eat outside, the sky would still be hot and oppressive, her father would join them for dessert and coffee, Guislaine would stop crying, her eyes would no longer be brimming with tears, "You know," Michelle would tell her mother, "I cry too, but my tears are dry," and her father would say, his fatigue making him detached, "You must tell that to the psychiatrist looking after you, your mother and I are worried about you enough as it is," a father, her own, apparently so detached, a tall young man with a serious mien, Papa, "In my dreams I was weeping dry tears that wouldn't stop flowing." Suddenly lenient, he would say, "Stop tormenting yourself, my dear, there are others to help you," the words, the phrases that haunted her, what they said, what they didn't say, why were they pestering her, as she walked she bent double under the pounding of their voices, she thought of spending a few hours in a school friend's room, there were always hooligans there, watching television all day and smoking hash, Michelle wasn't part of any group, the word "gang" filled her with loathing, when they had burgled an apartment together she had run away, terrified, someone had been hurt, blood everywhere, on the furniture, the rug, that wasn't how Guislaine and Paul had raised their daughters, her grandmother's perfume on the day she went to the hairdresser, the beseeching sweetness of that perfume, "Stay with us, Michelle, don't go, she'll be better after her exams," her father said, yet she hadn't phoned them when she was afraid, at the police station at three o'clock in the morning, she had fled to Raymonde, to Anna, Raymonde was Anna's mother, not hers, since that event, that night of terror, Guislaine held back the scalding tears at the roots of her eyelashes, "I've done everything for you and Liliane, even interrupted my own education, and you don't love me, I can't hate Raymonde, she's my best friend, but you should understand how I feel, Michelle, I'm jealous, I may as well admit it, and I'm ashamed of it," Michelle looked at her mother, feeling a sudden rush of love for her and her candour, "You know, I like going to a restaurant, just the two of us," she observed for the first time a wrinkle on her mother's brow, a wrinkle suddenly visible under the beautiful thick black hair, like hers but more richly textured, more voluptuous, she thought, they said so themselves, "No one could be as muddle-headed as Michelle," so incomplete, they also said, hadn't her father said or written that Michelle's was "a lost generation," their bewilderment could be seen in her abstracted gaze, in the texture of her hair which fell on her cheeks in limp waves, she had noticed it as she passed a store window, and the wrinkle on Guislaine's brow was caused by her, Michelle, "I'm the one who did that," she wanted to tell Guislaine, but she said nothing, merely looked at her mother with a surge of confused and hopeless love, thinking she would never love her enough, or as comfortably as she loved Raymonde, Alexandre, Anna, and Liliane whom she revered, Liliane embodied that pleasure in living Michelle would never know, not in this world, she would only have a vision of it through Liliane, she could admit nothing to them, weren't they envious, jealous, only Guislaine was bold enough to admit to her passionate vice – jealousy – "Yes, I'm jealous, I know it, be quiet, I don't want to hear you say that," she often shouted at Liliane, "You're tall, you're beautiful, and you look down your nose at everything, especially at morality, as if life were only that, I'm jealous because you're lazy and carefree, I've never had a minute's rest, with your father and the two of you, never, why shouldn't I be jealous, sad, empty, you all make me empty, sick with emptiness, most people are hideously jealous of others, they just don't admit it." "But Mama, your life is a success, you're a doctor and now you can go on with your research, what more do you want?" "To hear the last of you. Be quiet." And suddenly that wrinkle on her brow; the brow that had once considered everyone's needs was shadowed now by a wrinkle. Michelle's mother could not grow old so quickly, so soon, and these surges of confused and hopeless love bent her double as she walked, Guislaine, my mother, I have only Guislaine and one day I won't have her, they would eat outside, they would be intoxicated by the summer night, the city, they would find the strength to smile at their troubles as they drank wine happily, Michelle had started to eat a little again, she was no longer suffering from malnutrition as she had "when she was making all that fuss about Biafra," as they said, with no respect for her pain, she had been cured of that, of her tendency to die in the flesh of others, at school she had been told not to come back, she was too thin, Michelle would find the strength to smile at her troubles and her father would say, "What would Jung think of our little girl's dreams? What a lot of clouds in her thoughts, what do you think of yourself, Michelle, it's time you learned to laugh at yourself a little, like the rest of us," or else he would tell her – so motherly at times, like a woman – "Do you want to go shopping on Saturday and buy some new boots and jeans, would you like that?" and Guislaine would say, "Paul, you know Mich-

elle doesn't care about clothes, she's not like Liliane, always trying to seduce people, Michelle is so strange, she doesn't feel anything as others do, and she has so much musical talent, we're the
ones who don't understand her, we should simply tell ourselves
that she's unique, that she can't be compared to anyone else . . ."
It would be a warm and pleasant summer night, Michelle would
be alone with her mother, if the night was starry the next day
would also be fine, and Michelle would tell her mother, "I know
I made that wrinkle on your brow," or she would say nothing,
and they would be like two friends, Raymonde, Anna, like two
friends, silent and close, despite the churning of imminent collapse under their feet, Michelle thought. Michelle was no longer
bent double, but walking like everyone else, she thought, her fingers were very pale, very white in the light, slender fingers, one
day she might write music but you couldn't tell who she was
from watching her, from the front or the back, Raymonde had
sewn a button on her sweater the day they'd been picked up in a
stolen car, she didn't belong to those gangs of insolent, wild, un-
mannerly girls, why did she always fall into their traps, because
of Anna perhaps, who seemed to give in to all of them, for acid,
yet within her cold intelligence she gave in to no one, Michelle
thought, Raymonde had sewn a button on her sweater and the
metal button gleamed in the sun, hadn't Raymonde told her she
was too fragile for the Correctional Institute, that she couldn't
survive there, "Watch out for girls who are tougher than you,"
she had told her, in Anna's presence, and Anna had said nothing,
she was wearing a khaki shirt wide open over her flat breasts,
Michelle wondered if Anna was tough too, who she was, and
suddenly she knew, Anna's blonde head flying past at the level of
the trees, Anna bicycling through the air, the fire of that summer
day, Anna was following her own solitary ascent – towards what
place, what goal? – wasn't she more mystical than the others, less

materialistic? Michelle would have liked to follow her into that reclusive life where she hoped to hide herself, to know Anna and her cold intelligence, her mind that had already renounced everything to fix itself on a single vision of the world, sombre and final.

Anna was gliding past walls, past houses, she was hot, she was alive, Sylvie was still nothing but a babbling head in the hands of Peter, that familiar tamer of small children, Sylvie, Sylvie, as Anna had been in the past, but when he travelled and put Sylvie beside him in his silent, cushioned car, in the winter, when in the past, one endless summer, blazing and dry, he had dragged Anna along the roads of Los Angeles in a carrier fastened to his motorbike, the unleashed sky and roads, the smell of gas that poisoned your lungs and everywhere, water and sky, searing the eyelids like fire, all that intoxication belonged to Anna, bouncing like a ball in her carrier, a plush rabbit swaying from side to side with her, so tiny, Anna and the rabbit the same size, drifting away with Peter, the giant in this universe where everything escaped, fled, never to return, the bareness of landscapes as well as their abundance, the incandescence of the landscapes they had seen together whirling in Anna's soul like the galloping visions in Peter's gaze after he'd dropped acid yesterday, "Aren't you ashamed!" Raymonde exclaimed, snatching away Anna and her rabbit – two animals, victims of a single carnage, shuddering silently in Raymonde's arms, clinging to her, pleading but asking nothing, Anna's small warm head bare in the sun, the rabbit's ears still cool, perhaps it had rained that day, there had been such certainty in Anna's heart, I know you, Peter, you don't love my mother and me, and yet from the outside, the arms outstretched towards Raymonde and the tear-soaked rabbit, it might only have been Sylvie, her babbling head, but already that certitude existed – in Anna's heart, in Raymonde's – Peter, so gentle, so peaceful, Peter the conscientious objector, Peter the drifter, tender and sick, was fierce, cruel, he had nearly killed his little girl on his motorbike, but it wasn't his fault, no, it wasn't his fault, Raymonde said, the rabbit, Anna, Peter, Raymonde, all of them sitting calmly under the red sky, they would sleep by the fire and forget the journey, it was a delightful night, Anna and Peter were playing in the waves, kissing, forgiving one another, they're so small at that age, yes, she had fallen asleep against Peter's shoulder, his beard touching her forehead. In the winter Peter would take Sylvie out in his car, soundless in the winter silence, huddled in a fur coat, inside there would be a shape called Sylvie, a face, two troubled eyes, and Peter would say "Darling, Daddy's darling, my love," and the eyes would open wide, limpid and blue as Peter's own, winter would have no movement, no sounds, and the visions of the past would be scattered in the distance, muddled only in Anna's memory, in her awareness, running, galloping all alone, like Peter's visions in the past when he dragged Anna over the roads, the world and its wars, the world and its barbarism flipping past in his eye while he shouted, drifting, drifting away, and seemed to triumph over everything, even Anna's fear as she bounced like a ball in her carrier, even the love of Raymonde whom he would often beat, hitting her on the head, one day he'd break a chair over her back and afterwards tell her, kneeling, sobbing, "It's always the innocent we hurt, you know that," kneeling before Raymonde between ocean and sky, Raymonde whom he would beat again, humiliate, while Anna's rigid little brow rose up against him, she would never forgive, never erase the insult, Anna who had seen Peter in his new garden, his new house, with Sylvie, had seen him for the last time perhaps. Anna glided past walls, past

houses, the wheels of her bicycle glittering in the sun, her brow
and hair were drenched with sweat, a sweat-stained garment on
a chair in an empty space, that was her last image of Philippe, a
lifetime in just a few months at Philippe's side, and then, suddenly, nothing but that empty space and the memory of a
sweat-stained garment, it was shortly before she went home to
Raymonde, Alexandre, her dog, her birds, shortly before what
they thought was a return, a happy ending to a bad business,
and weren't they right? Sitting on this chair against the white
wall of his office, looking again for an untouched spot on his
arm for the needle, Philippe said, "How self-centered – for a
rush, a moment of oblivion, men like me, who seem to be leading normal lives, put up with being searched, being violated at
the border." She heard the voice that came from so far away,
dreaming that she had raised up her body in the silence, her
anus transformed into a mysterious, afflicted hiding place, they
raped you with their eyes, yes, but she had raised up her body
for their silent torture, she would not bend, not to anyone, suddenly all that remained of Philippe was a sweat-stained garment
on a chair and the memory of a walk in Paris, where he had told
her as he lifted her up in his arms, "Why did you follow me,
child, go home to your mother, I feel as old as Europe, you
mustn't give your living soul to dead souls, you'll see, dead
men and dead souls exist even in life, don't fall victim to
them," and she had hated him for speaking like that, didn't he,
more than the others, know the depth of her solemn defiance,
then he didn't love her, or not any more or less than the other
delinquents who came to his place to sleep and eat, they had
closed their own doors when Philippe said, "Come to my
place," and he dreamed, for all of them, of a future city, he had
drawn up the plans for it, but hadn't he loved and cherished
Anna, his little Anna, her obstinate brow like Raymonde's, with

the same detachment, the same stubborn faith, and she was so insolent, so obstinate, thinking only of her own pleasure, the same pleasure she felt as she glided past walls, past houses, a summer breeze cooling her neck, her hair, the pleasure that was her own pleasure at being alive, far from them all, with no attachments, and with Raymonde, as with Philippe, there were still these sweet ties of affection, of love, and their tenacious hold, to live with them, tame and trusting, wasn't that what they demanded in spite of everything, no, they demanded nothing, didn't even say, "Come and go as you wish," they no longer dared to say what they felt in their love or their sorrow, for Anna had brushed them aside, hadn't Philippe promised to cut down on drugs if Anna lived with him, he was prematurely old, he said, he had rediscovered his youth in Anna, her illumination, it was while thinking of her that he drew up the plans for a future city – for her, for all of them – drifting among the drifters, he had a foreboding that one day they would need shelter, warmth, "You and your friends won't always be on the road, Anna, you must stop moving away from us, stop punishing yourselves, all the drifters on earth are like you, they have the same sense of exile," it wasn't only heroin that made him so understanding as he stroked Anna's hair, it was that illumination he talked about so often, love, others might have accused him of leading minors astray but Anna was highly mature, fully aware, she herself admitted the soundness of his thinking, from the first days of her life, that moment when she began defying Peter, defending her own rights and Raymonde's, but was her foreboding fair, perhaps Peter was just a father like so many others of his generation. Later, Raymonde had taught her to respect him, her father had been a conscientious objector, he had not killed, her father was an artist suffering from the solitude, the exasperation that were his fate, there was nothing to prove that

Peter was truly evil, in the past, when he was nothing but a drifter, hadn't his style of life, the way he was living then, been much the way she was living now? Who knows whether he hadn't struggled, suffered as she herself was suffering, in the same silence, "You should write to your mother, Anna, tell her you're living with me, haven't you thought how worried she must be?" and Anna's obstinate brow was lifted towards Philippe, one day she would write to Raymonde, "It's me, Anna, I'm alive, a man is taking care of me," that would be the first victory for Philippe, to whose authority and supervision she must submit, she would leave him, where was Philippe now, what had become of his love for Anna while she was gliding past walls, past houses, did he know, Anna wondered, that she had only lived with him, under his roof, for her own pleasure, it was less cold than out in the street, in his bed she was warm, strange that he showed so little judgement about her childish greed, he was always smiling, his delicate hands on his worktable and his wooden chair, perhaps he was still sitting there, alone now, holding a syringe, thinking of his parents whose death had been a pointless sacrifice, when he, Philippe, was still there, Anna didn't understand his obsessive exile, nor the wandering that was his curse, didn't he look like a meticulous, hardworking man, the only worry visible to Anna's soul – a worry she had appropriated for herself, she thought – was that he lived only for others, even when he conceived of a future life he thought of the space, the freedom of movement, that Anna and her friends might need tomorrow, Anna too would dream of a simple, elementary life, along with modern comforts, that was how she broke away from Philippe, voluntarily, lifting her obstinate brow towards him, a man who would be deserted from now on, left as she had seen him for the last time, sitting on his chair, wiping his brow with a garment already stained with sweat, she had loved his presence, his cultivation, his sensuality which had awakened her own, and in her greed she had thought, Philippe and everything he is, everything he possesses, is my transfusion of life, of blood, that's how they act, after all, they take everything we are, but who knows if she wasn't deluding herself about Philippe, Anna was strong, Philippe hadn't sensed the madness behind her concealed authority, which had frightened Peter so much, like Peter she was capable of wounding, of inflicting pain, she had loved Tommy's black skin, she loved Philippe because he was one of those creatures who are marked, scarred, who seem to have no skin left, only the blood flowing under his hardened soul and the bones of his face, she watched him working for hours at a time, wondering how someone like him thought, how he considered things, he loved though she did not, he would say, "We must change the world, for you," while she was inert and refused any change, wasn't she guilty above all of a monstrous inertia that she mentioned to no one, he was creative whereas she despised art, she merged her identity with other people's, she even refused to respond to beauty, her mother said, Philippe thought only of her, defencelessly she ate at his table, criticizing everything, like the other delinquents, trampling his secrets, his life, his inner kingdom, and that greed, the greed of Anna whom he loved, seemed to please him, "It's easy to see that you love life," he would say; "What will, what determination you put into your behaviour, into all your acts, what furor!" Anna glided past walls, past houses, Philippe's features moving away from her, was she not guilty of wounding them, transfiguring them, would she not escape only when she had grasped the significance of this painful existence, it is not enough merely to exist, Philippe would say, they all deserved a better life, without all the poisons in the air and time, a better life, Anna thought, the summer breeze caressed her brow, her hair, the drops of sweat on her temples, to live, Anna thought, and Michelle stopped, her books under her arm, before the yard of a boys' school, empty except for a puppy playing with its master, "I'm trying to teach him something while there's still time," said the man to Michelle, "but he doesn't listen to me," the dog and his master were running gaily, in a tree a cat was watching them, seeming to want to jump into the yard but hesitating, watching first the puppy, then the man, condescendingly, at times it shrank back slightly, "I'm teaching him obedience," the man repeated, "but he never listens to me," Michelle, leaning against an iron fence, watched the man, the puppy and the cat in the tree all rushing to her senses like a summer whirlwind, it was like the fine light down on her arms, her legs, when the sun shone on it, though ever since she and Anna had parted in the bright sun the light had been declining, but so slowly, "He's just a few months old," the man told Michelle, touched by the small creature quivering with joy beside him, "He'll never learn to bring me my newspaper, like dogs in the movies." "No, he'll never learn that," Michelle agreed, and it soothed her that this unknown man had started talking to her, just a few more streets and she would be home, she came this way in autumn and winter, the deserted schoolyard was an invitation to linger there, but in autumn, in winter, a pile of dead leaves, frost-covered, in the snow or rain, would draw her like a bed, she could have slept there, transfixed in the earth's tears, transfixed by the frost and cold, never awakened again, and she would have been forgotten there, with no sorrow, no nostalgia, perhaps, for didn't everyone need to rest sealed in the earth, the cold ground that was the source of everything must be waiting for her, a bit of wind and a rain of flowers would fall from the tree, Michelle thought, the cat was leaning heavily on its branch watching the man and the dog, who had started to run again, paying no attention to

Michelle, to her thoughts under her dishevelled hair, but the summer whirlwind was there still, the hot air lurking everywhere, under Michelle's sweater, on her nape, one November evening Liliane had come here to fetch her, she had fallen asleep on her bed of icy leaves, "Mama's looking for you everywhere, come on," Liliane had said, helping her sister up, she had taken her in her arms as if to carry her, Michelle thought, perhaps she had carried her, saying in her ear, "I always know you may be here, ever since that time you picked up the old man and brought him home to sleep, that was nice, you know, but Mama can't take in all the old men you find on the street, living like bums, you wouldn't want to be found out here frozen for good, really frozen, I don't know why you like to come and curl up in these dirty grey corners where it's so cold," from then on she felt that Liliane could find her anywhere, if it happened that she didn't wake up, or if she fell asleep "frozen" in this schoolyard where no one came at night, but everyone was gilded by the sun, perhaps the glacial damp wouldn't come back within these walls, no, here, today, she hadn't thought of coming to lie beside the wall, not even to rest her face against the hot cement of the schoolyard, listening to her pulse pounding wildly in her temples, telling herself, if my heart beats once more my head, my ears will explode. In the summer Liliane would have taken her to the corner for an orangeade, asking her to wait while she finished a tennis match, in winter she would have prepared a hot cup of soup, a bath, she would have rubbed her down from head to toe as she had when Michelle was little, telling her, "Before you were born I was waiting for you and I wanted you more than all the others, and Mama was very jealous of my love for you," she would have let her sleep at her side, holding her hand in the dark, when Michelle was cold she would lie on top of her to warm her, telling her again, their cheeks touching, "I don't want anything to happen to you, I don't want you to fall like a partridge shot down in the woods," and as the flood of dry tears was no longer flowing Michelle thought as she fell asleep, I think I'm glad I'm falling asleep, tomorrow morning I think I'll have forgotten what draws me to the schoolyard, there was a peace, a sort of void amid the fragrance of rotting leaves, the old vagabonds themselves like to die there, just a few more blocks and Michelle would be home, their home but a safe place still, she would be there, they wouldn't be able to say that she was absent, that they still didn't know where she was, she would kiss her grandmother, play the piano for her, no, she wouldn't play for her grandmother, she often had a feeling of paralysis in her left hand, "It's all in your imagination," said Paul, the feeling overwhelmed her, made her sick, she would eat alone with her mother perhaps, once a week they ate together outside, Michelle was still walking, her books under her arm, her elbow had grazed a boy around twenty who was pushing a baby carriage, you couldn't see the child, it seemed buried under bubbles of silk deep down in its travelling cradle, but the boy was wearing a bathing suit as red as Anna's T-shirt, and he wore a sailor's hat, Michelle had grazed him with her elbow as she passed and now the boy was behind her, whistling, she could no longer see or hear him but the air was still misty, red, a harsh colour that evoked Anna soaring past on her bicycle, past the trees, suddenly Michelle was there, her trembling hands playing with the house keys, her father and grandmother who were talking in the living room hadn't seen her come in, perhaps Guislaine had been delayed at the hospital by some emergency, or else she'd forgotten Michelle, Paul was trying to persuade his mother to go to the dentist, "Of course, Mother, I know they're going to pull several teeth, but it'll just be a local anaesthetic, then you can come here to rest for a few days." "And what if I don't wake up?" asked the old lady, Paul tried to convince his mother and the tone of his voice irritated Michelle, he was patient, nobly patient, as if he were talking to Liliane about her sexual problems, or to Michelle about cocaine, the dangers that threatened their lives, a complication in the delicate machinery that was so quick to break down, each vigorous heartbeat followed by the same death, the same ending, if Guislaine was delayed again because of some complication, Michelle must wait, in this brief time Liliane would already have opened the refrigerator, she was always hungry, and scattered cigarette ashes all around her, where was Liliane, "a real cat in heat," Guislaine would say, "always in love with some girl – didn't she try to seduce her babysitter when she was only twelve?" Where was Liliane, perhaps she wouldn't come, they saw her so seldom, at times Paul's voice could be heard, his footsteps, he must be hovering around his mother, surrounding her with advice, protection, "There's nothing to be afraid of, Mother," he said, "you'll come here afterwards for a few days' rest, we'll take care of you." "But I don't want to," said the old lady, "I don't like to bother people." "You know very well I have other things to do besides argue on and on with you about this, I haven't finished my article." "You have your Ph.D.," said the old lady, "why do you always have to be writing and writing?" Michelle was listening to the Beethoven concerto that she could sing by heart, but they would hear nothing, she thought, the Beethoven concerto was there, joyful and sweet, for her alone, like nightfall in the school-yard, the man and his dog playing in a shadow theatre, "I don't want the children to see me without my new teeth," said the old lady, "You know it can happen at my age, Paul, people simply don't wake up again," Michelle was taking off her sweater, lying down on her bed, "I thought I heard a noise," they said, "We must water those poor plants," Michelle's grandmother walked across the living room, watered the plants, with the exhilaration of the Beethoven concerto Michelle's heart was beating wildly, irregularly, beating in her skull, she thought, under her hair, it was electrifying, her heart beating, beating, and Liliane wasn't there, there was a bottle of gin under her bed, Liliane never drank from it but she liked to annoy her father, Michelle was frightened and thirsty, "I've never liked the idea of putting people to sleep in order to cause them pain," said Michelle's grandmother. "Not at all, you'll feel better afterwards," said Paul, his patience was running out but he was trying to control himself, after all, his mother was an old woman, and widowed now, she was becoming cantankerous, when she came home from vacation she had complained about the heat, about "those nasty, noisy old men," she said, Paul didn't have time to take care of all the women in the house – Guislaine, his mother, Liliane, Michelle – a man has his own life too, and his career to worry about, with all the ideas about domination that torment women today, they don't even have a sense of humour, he thought, they don't understand men, don't know how to love them as they once did, the old lady was watering the plants, complaining about the cost of living, "and ungrateful children who cost their parents so much," the gin invigorated Michelle, who had got up and was now walking in her mother's room, Guislaine had time to sleep, didn't she carry on her secret correspondence early in the morning, write in her diary, Michelle wasn't allowed there, in that space that didn't belong to her, but she was there, sneakily insinuating herself into this place, her stomach filled with alcohol she couldn't digest, one day they would all go and live in the country, yes, one day they would leave behind the dying life of the cities, and there, "We'll take all the books we haven't had time to read during the year," Guislaine said, it would be the dawn of a new life, Michelle thought, the genesis, another age, genesis, she liked that inaccessible word, but she had already drunk too much of this revolting stuff, Guislaine's daughters shouldn't drink, shouldn't take drugs, nothing, Guislaine had planned to go out with Michelle that evening, because everything was ready – her elegant leather shoes, the matching handbag – Michelle's heart was beating wildly, didn't Guislaine chide Raymonde for not caring about clothes, "She'll end up looking like her delinquents," she would say, her shoes, her leather bag, her perfume, these objects and their peaceful, mundane life were waiting for Guislaine, were concealed in her place, in the bedroom, forbidden to come in here, and Michelle's heart was beating wildly, her legs quivering with weakness, so that was the alcoholic release everyone talked about – a wave of images, of sensations struck at her nerves, I'm sick, she thought, I'm going to vomit and then everybody will know, they would come up and touch her, she was caught in her body's distress like a butterfly in a spiderweb, the butterfly, the fabric of the web were scorched by the sun, she was no longer moving but awaiting a rescue that wouldn't come, Liliane, Liliane, the delicate shoes, the leather bag, yes, they liked going out together, they'd go out together in the evening, but her father, her grandmother were beside her now, asking what was going on, she was forbidden to come in here, into Guislaine's room, didn't she know, why did she look so frightened, like someone about to die, they dragged her to the bathroom asking why, why, she couldn't say anything, "My pet," said her grandmother, holding her in her arms, and Michelle thought, that's what is known as pity, degrading pity, why must they subject me to it, but they were there asking questions, trying to understand, surrounding her with their solicitude as well as their suspicions, "Michelle, why won't you talk to us?" her father was preparing to wash her face, they were so close, suddenly, that Michelle smelled her father's breath on her cheeks, his gaze, tender and moist like hers, was lost in her bright pupils, there was an animal bond between this pretentious father and Michelle, who thought of herself only as a dizzying failure, or if he wasn't pretentious at least he was never in the wrong, he didn't drink, didn't smoke, and he never made mistakes, why am I not out on the street, she thought, the bond between him and me is intolerable, why am I not out on the street, rolling joints with friends indifferent to everything, so indifferent that they stare straight ahead seeing nothing, you saw them everywhere, haggard, indifferent, sitting on park benches or on steps, stretching out there, as if on the edge of the abyss, as if their somnolent legs, their arms, were separate from the rest of their bodies, as if they were cut off from their awareness of life, it felt good, Michelle thought, dizzy from her drowsy contemplation of the void, she had to sustain the moist and tender gaze of her father, her father who could talk about everything, excited by his certainties and the sound of his own solemn voice, the voice of an educator, a pedagogue, as if he were always giving a lecture, her grandmother was brushing her hair, familiarly, for they were family and, who knows, perhaps this soulless familiarity was their way of expressing love, "I'm going to call the doctor," said Paul, and Michelle thought, I hate them, I hate them, but I let them touch me, suddenly Liliane appeared, exclaiming, "Leave Michelle alone, you're always upsetting her," with Liliane she would soon be free of their artful caresses, Liliane said, "I'm going to wash her, I love her, you don't." "Lesbian," said her father furiously, "keep your hands off our daughter," but he had said nothing, no murmur, no sound came from his lips, his gaze, still moist and tender, contemplated his daughters as if he were contemplating a disaster, but he didn't utter a word, Liliane was running Michelle's bath, she and some friends belonged to an ecology group, she said, if they didn't think about saving the planet, who else would do it? The conversation between Paul and his mother continued, Michelle could feel her heart fluttering in her chest, if hash cost seventy-five dollars an ounce how did they afford it, "These days several people get together to buy what they want," said Paul, and his voice sounded gloomy and unhappy, "The girls are turning out badly and I'm very sorry about it," said the old lady, "You can't live without religious beliefs, everything else follows from that." Paul explained to his mother that above all Michelle needed care, they never mentioned Liliane, Liliane represented forbidden sensuality, the anomaly of joy triumphant, at twelve she had already been six feet tall, today she seemed to want to destroy you with her ideas, her words, ironic words that wounded him, but Michelle was more vulnerable, with care and attention she would be cured, all the knots of sterile anguish that separated him from her, his child, her physical appearance was sometimes so deplorable he was disgusted, "No one will want to wash your clothes, Michelle, they're falling to pieces, like you," they're going to throw me on the scrap heap, she thought, Liliane said as she was bathing her, "If you're having a bad trip, they mustn't find out." Liliane's words gradually drew Michelle from her lethargy, her solitude, she was no longer lying down, as in winter, breathing with difficulty on a pile of leaves, among poor people and tramps numb with cold who asked, "What are you doing here with us, the destitute and the dying?" She knew, however, that her place was with them, even if they were less certain, "Some day you'll play music all day long," said Liliane, "and I'll teach," Michelle's gaze was blurred and distant, "Go back to your nest," they said, and yet, who knows, one day they were going to give up, on this pile of frozen leaves, die without even a muffled groan, in this cold where everything broke, or bent, without parents or friends,

"You can wear my velvet jeans, we'll turn up the cuffs, what are you afraid of, you can see I'm here beside you," and Guislaine had stopped her car under the trees, the chilled air inside the car cooled her for a moment against the blazing heat outside, even though her silk scarf was sticking to her neck, she could very well give the scarf to Michelle, after all, Michelle liked everything her mother wore, it would be something else for when she slept outside in the parks, like a vagabond, winter and summer, a vagabond, or Michelle would sell the scarf for a little dope, no, it was all unreal, the city smoke in summer, the sky full of oil fumes, the patient's condition seemed stable, it would have been more honest to let Paul know she didn't want to come home before five o'clock, no emergency, if the condition remained stable, yes, but would he be condemned in six months, a year, this city smoke that destroyed the children's health, slowly, slowly weakening their minds, their bodies, she would put a little more money aside and they would go away, they would finally have time to read, as for her newspaper, she opened it, then immediately closed it, her fatigue made everything incoherent, you had to wait so long, Guislaine thought, before knowing how to acquire for yourself the basic right to live according to your own desires and not those of others, a silk scarf around Michelle's grimy neck, no, what's the use of giving in to these generous feelings, people always take advantage of them, Michelle wouldn't have the scarf, Michelle shouldn't receive anything, not even the money she was constantly demanding for her music lesions, her books, as for cigarettes, she would forbid them all to smoke in her presence, she had opened a book, she understood nothing in the tissue of sober, silent words, but hadn't Paul told her to read this excellent study, even in their student days she didn't like the philosophical works he forced her to read, what dismal hostility in these pages, she thought, what was she waiting for here – in her air-conditioned car, when it was a blazing summer day for everyone outside – wasn't it the end of her captivity among them? Tonight she would push away Paul and his embrace, his punctual, straightforward caresses, she would tell him, I want to go off alone, with the girls, to the country, I'm dying of this life without passion, without the all-consuming love we once knew, I'll go away with Liliane and Michelle, but I have to admit I feel no maternal love for them, maybe I'm mistaken, if she no longer enjoyed the book open on her lap it was because she was weary, last night the words she was reading at Paul's side had reassured her, made her feel more proud, she thought as she read them, now that's just what I am, what I think, how well this is written, these men's brows, these eyes, like Paul's, have absorbed so much learning for me, all human knowledge, these eyes, tender and moist like Paul's, but no, in the cold, structured words there was only dismal hostility, where was the intuition, the acuity that would match her heart's nostalgia, these words, these books were her enemies, they had excited her because she loved Paul, or had loved him once, his smooth self-satisfaction when he was talking about writers he admired, one day she would be indispensable, but somewhere else – in Brazil the sick and the dead in hospital were everyday occurrences, as punctual as Paul's caresses, she would go to Brazil, they need volunteer physicians, she would be indispensable, her professional qualities would be recognized, and her intransigence, too, indispensable, "Mama, I can't live without you," Michelle said, but the words were as heavy as a captive's chain, she was hovering again, like a small animal, sniffing the fragrance of your flesh, your clothes, "You're so beautiful, Mama, so sexy," these gentle, languorous wild creatures, children, Michelle, Liliane, no, Liliane already loved other women and she was jealous of them, jealous, jealous, she thought, biting her lips, but she would forbid her to live in her house with a girlfriend, she still had that power, and Paul, their secret dictatorship, their complicity, they could still say, "As long as you're under our roof you must obey us," Michelle had a passion for Wagner, where did it come from? They were just intellectuals like so many others, good parents, but suddenly they felt they had no goal in life, with their bitter knowledge, it was the hospital, yes, the hospital drained all her energy, when did she have time to think, to mull over the chaos, the splendour that was Michelle, Michelle whom they sent to a psychiatrist to appease her fury, "It's the only solution," said Paul, but was he right? At eight she already had forebodings about cataclysms, refused to go to school, somewhere far away, later that day, she would say, there would be an earthquake, a subterranean overthrowing of life, yes, she foresaw everything, basically she hadn't changed, Guislaine thought, Michelle's colliding, chaotic universe embraced Wagner's ardour just as yesterday it had embraced earthquakes, geological catastrophes, just as yesterday she had told her sister, "Don't go to school, the earth might blow up today," the atomic volcano was there, inhabiting all her thoughts, that was how she had grown up, in terror, and there were others like her – Michelle, like so many others, Guislaine thought, had the gift for martyrdom of those with abnormally acute senses, she was a child of her generation, why were they so worried about her, "She must be brought back to serenity," said Paul, to a comfortable, outdated sort of life, that deceitful life that no longer existed except for a few people, and yet at her age you had fun, went dancing at discothèques, liked pleasing boys, an outdated, comfortable life, yes, Guislaine would give her the scarf, take her to a restaurant, please her, she had neglected her so often in the past because of her studies, they would go to the country to live, forget these difficult years, Guislaine had closed the book on her lap, from time to time she opened the car window, the hot air, the sky full of oil fumes reminded her for a moment that outside there was chaos, that her idleness was coming to an end, for soon it would be five o'clock, she lit a cigarette, then immediately threw it onto the street, no, she mustn't do that, she would set an example, she wouldn't smoke, either alone or in their presence, "Mama, you're so beautiful, so sexy," the men she attracted on the street seemed crude to her, beautiful, sexy, Michelle's image was pursuing her, she no longer attracted men, didn't have time for that, she thought, Raymonde went through life seemingly imperturbable, insensitive to other people's desires, bound only, so it seemed, to her daughter's malaise, to the concerns of youth, was that a life? – to live that way, austere, stripped bare since Alexandre had taken off, "Michelle is in a perpetual state of regression," the specialists said of her sickness, but even though they kept on auscultating her, with the shameful attentions of psychology, of medicine, Guislaine thought, didn't Michelle's soul possess that quality of being inalienable, while all those around her were holding back their prisoners' cries, myself included, thought Guislaine, sighing, are they not victims of our weariness, of our cowardice, it was already late, time to think of going home, another cigarette after all, perhaps, she was alone, already imagining her repulsion when Michelle came to huddle in her arms, she would offer her the scarf quickly, to get rid of her, what wickedness made her feel this way, sometimes they found some miserable creature whom Michelle had hidden in her room, who knows, there too perhaps Guislaine was jealous, jealous of Michelle's pity for the dregs of society, pity was part of the plenitude of love and was Guislaine still capable of loving, no, perhaps, she thought, with Michelle and her troubles with acid you could never be sure, never live your life peaceably, as in the past, or tell yourself, tonight at dinnertime we'll have a normal conversation, we'll go to the library

together as we did when her father was reading them Alexandre Dumas to put them to sleep at night, they still loved one
another then, didn't torment one another so much, didn't spend
the whole night fighting bitterly over the children's education, it
would be a beautiful summer night, leaning on the arm of
Michelle, of Liliane, she would be confident, talkative, happy,
she would not yet have known that shame, that heartbreak, she
would open the door, Michelle would throw her arms around
her neck saying, "I'm squeaky clean, Mama, so I can go out with
you, look behind my ears if you want," Michelle's sticky fingers
when she touched you, you never knew where she'd been,
Liliane was silent, looking lovingly at her sister, "I don't know
where she was, I've brought her back, that's all, look after her or
I'll take her away," the threat in these words, the smile made
cutting by the anxieties of love, if she learned any more about
Liliane, wouldn't stagnating jealousy make her suffer even more,
a feeling so shameful, so vile for a mother, she must be the only
mother who felt that way, so deeply, Michelle's sticky fingers
caressing her nape, "Mama, I saw your shoes, your leather bag,
I love you, you're so elegant I could eat you up," "Don't talk to
me like that, go and wash your face," the evening would be hot
and heavy, often when the weather was fine, on summer nights,
they stayed up all night gazing at the stars, simply relaxing
together, Michelle's arm or Liliane's against her own, in silent,
serene meditation, and suddenly Michelle's slender fingers scattering over her the filth of the street, the neglect, the misery of
the cities, it was intolerable, who else would tolerate that, it
must be late because, mechanically, as she did every night, she
had come home, was listening to her keys jingling in her jacket
pocket, on her lips, in her nostrils, there was still that musty
smell of smoke, of fuel oil, yes, she would sign the ecological
petition Liliane had shown her that morning, these criminals

who blackened the sky blackened everything, yielding to the ineluctable panic that one day we would all die, the fatality of a universal negligence that would descend on everyone, pleading with them to renounce any attempt to live, she too, Guislaine, was a victim of the cowardice of these criminals who were jealous of innocence, of beauty, this was one revolt she could still share with her daughters, but who knows, in this combat perhaps they were all, weak or powerful, all vanquished, they would be expelled from the earth they had impoverished, wounded, as they deserved to be, the sky was blue and hot, you could hear the Beethoven concerto even on the street, the neighbours would complain, why didn't Michelle use the earphones given her by her father who didn't like noise, music in the house, the earphones and their wires resembled, Guislaine thought, the branched structure of glass tubing that allowed transfusions of serum, of blood in the lives of the seriously ill, the hospital, yes, that was it, the hospital was draining her energy, wearing away her nerves, was that the purpose of life, that wearing away, the slowness of all the forms of mourning perpetuated in us, in them, which she became more and more aware of every day, "The neighbours are going to complain again," said Guislaine as she came in, but the girls were probably in their rooms at the back, this apartment was too big, "functional" said Paul, someone had thought of the plants, a note on the kitchen table told Guislaine that her husband was out but would be back soon, and thus everything was a warning, a solicitude, the signs of captivity were still present, even in Paul's handwriting, in appearance a restrained handwriting but for Guislaine, who suddenly deciphered it, the mark of an insolence she alone could read, "After Mother goes to the dentist next week, as you know, she'll be spending a few days with us, you know we can't leave her by herself when she's in pain," that's how they love you, Guislaine thought – running to satisfy their greedy needs, men or women, or children – she draped her linen jacket on a chair, she valued that jacket, when she was reading or smoking by herself in the summer, in her glacial car, the cold, the coolness that is, during the teeming, grimy, germ-filled summer, the cold, the chosen coolness when outside it seemed as if the trees, the pavement, the people themselves were writhing in the poisoned air, she remembered a young woman who had lost her shoe as she was walking, a little farther on, in another street where she had followed her, Guislaine had noticed her throw her head back, in a gesture of weakness perhaps, was she going to faint, while a grey pigeon flew across the sky, thus did summer sweep by, in a flash, Guislaine had thought, in her car, observing the bird that seemed to her to be suspended in the hot air, as she herself was when she joined in the commotion of the street, and suddenly it was late, Guislaine was once more a captive of the voices, the murmurs coming from the back bedrooms, Liliane and Michelle were probably talking softly to each other, they would fall silent when they saw their mother, they were there, sitting at the foot of the bed, united as they so often were by their mute complicity, suddenly silent because Guislaine had just come in, or changing the subject as Liliane was doing, addressing her mother derisively, "Did somebody's pancreas hold you up, Guislaine?" and that name, her Christian name, in Liliane's mouth, the girl abused her constantly with her words, her retorts, and why had Guislaine been so incautious as to mention at the table, the previous day, her concern about a patient with a disease of the pancreas, "I'm your mother," said Guislaine, "you should speak to me with respect," "I do speak respectfully, Mama," said Liliane, looking her mother straight in the eye, her gaze was irritating, Guislaine thought, spirited, inconsiderate, she doesn't veil her thoughts in the least, Guislaine reflected as she submitted to it, Liliane was watching her mother and stroking Michelle's cheek – that little hollow in her cheeks, she said, must be filled out, rounded – with her strong, square fingertips, and Guislaine had shut her eyes as if that light mechanical touch had wounded her, after all, if Liliane was already spending half her time in a girls' commune – almost all of them children who had already left home – she could kick her out before she turned eighteen, she would soon be accepted by an art school, she would see less of her, it was unbearable to think that this girl, already so sturdy and tall, would continue to grow, would be a painter or sculptor, the skill of her body, her hands seemed formidable already, but no, they were proud of Liliane, Liliane was always successful, what a pity she had this one flaw, was it a form of deviant sexuality as Paul said, or an overflowing lust for life, quite healthy and natural? Was it a calamity to have a daughter like Liliane, so different from others, different at least from the comparisons she could draw among her fellow doctors, no teacher's daughter was like her, or lived like her either, her exaltation was so physical, yes, she wouldn't have wanted to share her concern with anyone else, not even Raymonde, even in the enamel of her teeth you could sense that will to seduce, to please, thought Guislaine, who avoided her daughter's eyes as she drew closer to Michelle and enfolded her in her arms, gently extracting her from her sister's influence, repeating that's what it is, it's jealousy, how shameful, and as she was thus, consciously and blatantly, separating Michelle from Liliane, she thought of the canoe trip they had once taken together, during a holiday in Switzerland when the three of them had been alone, without Paul, who was working on his dissertation, those dazzling days came back often in her dreams, Liliane, Michelle gliding gently over the brown water of the lake, without words, the coolness of the water, of the night falling over the treetops, hadn't numbed them, so close to one another, the water lapping at their small craft lost in the middle of the night, that their hands, their feet touched as, scarcely moving, they seemed to be rowing, their arms, their hands sketching gestures above the water, when in reality, Guislaine thought, the silent water was drawing them on, out of their way, towards the centre of the black and peaceful lake, where they had waited for nightfall, united by the same anxious silence, Liliane, Michelle, Guislaine, their small craft undulating gently on the brown water of the lake, she suddenly awakened from this dream, her forehead soaked in sweat, she felt that Liliane and Michelle were no longer in the canoe as it glided on alone past the squat forest that bordered the lake, if they were still in the canoe the shadows of the trees were concealing them, you couldn't make out their silhouettes, and yet Guislaine was still on the lake, struggling alone against the resounding curtain of all that water threatening to carry her so far away from them, the dream was subsiding, scattering into a trivial occurrence with Liliane introducing a girlfriend to her mother, calling the friend her mistress, getting down on her knees before her as she was doing now, tenderly, before Michelle, telling her that the velvet trousers were still too long, they must be cut off, and Guislaine held Michelle against her breast saying, "Come, let's go and eat," not asking Liliane what she would do tonight, afraid of what she might find out, still feeling on her nape, as she was leaving with Michelle, Liliane's insolent gaze following after her, murmuring for her alone, "I love women and you're jealous, jealous of all the erotic experience you didn't have when you were my age, jealous, jealous," but Liliane was saying to her mother that she was going to an ecology meeting tonight, "another meeting with nothing but women," said Guislaine dryly, but Liliane, who was humming the Beethoven concerto rather tunelessly, perhaps hadn't heard her, you could no longer swim in our rivers, or eat the fish, Guislaine listened to her absently as she freshened up her face, telling herself, I probably judge her too harshly, above all I mustn't let her see that I'm judging her, she'll go out of her way to live a life that's even more amoral. "You can come with us, you know," she said mildly, thinking at the same time of the bond of chaste friendship between herself and Raymonde, Raymonde, Guislaine, inseparable once, no, in the dream the canoe was drifting by itself, you couldn't see them any more, past the squat forests that bordered the distant mysterious lake, a landscape they would never see again, perhaps, in this lifetime, and in this personal room where Guislaine, before she left that morning, had put out her bag and shoes for her evening with Michelle, these traces that filled Guislaine with such disgust, the traces of Michelle's sticky fingers were there, everywhere, on her books, on the diary she hadn't time to write in, her solitary retreat. Michelle, her throbbing body, her obscure ills brought on by drugs, all the misery she had absorbed elsewhere, throughout the day, these vestiges of Michelle came rushing at her once again, overwhelming her, accusing her as if she were whispering in her ear, with the acrid odour of her breath, "You don't love me, you don't love me enough." Had Raymonde not confided to Guislaine – she who confided so little – how much Anna's fury, her silent hostility sometimes saddened her, even when she was hoping to please her, to move her even, by taking her to the land of her ancestors, Anna's indifference, like her indifference to the Boudin reproduction in her room, said Raymonde, drove away any hope of reconciliation with her mother's past, as if she were still thinking of the dizzying roads she had once travelled with her father, flung about on his motorbike, roughly handled on the Los Angeles roads under the bright blue daytime sky, the blazing sky of evening, Guislaine, Liliane, Michelle were gliding across the brown water of a lake, adrift in their canoe, while Raymonde, Anna, were travelling by train towards the light of the south of France, Raymonde contemplating painfully, for the first time, Anna's rigid brow, closed to everything, the opacity of this child wrapped in her own silence, and the sullen fold at the corner of her mouth that seemed to say, leave me alone, leave me alone, I'm somewhere else, and where I am there's no life, only a sorrowful void, oh! Leave me alone, and close to Raymonde there were other couples, mothers and daughters, happy to be together, a little girl of Anna's age, dressed like her in white shorts, a striped blue cotton sweater, wearing the same Levi's shoes – for these children of well-to-do families had to be able to recognize one another, to be aware – even in the way they adorned themselves with seemingly crude simplicity – of that flutter of privilege, of a social likeness that belonged only to them, still under their mothers' wings, the little girl who was like Anna in that one respect sat beside the window drawing, touchingly but without imagination, huge red hearts which she then placed on her mother's lap, wasting a good many sheets of paper and a great deal of ink, as if such waste too were dictated, Raymonde thought, by the ostentation that she shared with Anna's class, in which privilege declared itself by its luxury, blank sheets of paper, red, white, green pencils, there were plenty of them, and in this first-class coach Anna, like the little French girl, might have shared the same range of colours, like their clothes or their haircuts, Anna, unlike the little girl, was not drawing hearts eloquent with love for her adoring and adored mother, her hands rested on her bare knees, thin and glacial, Raymonde had thought, as if parched by the cold, by death, those hands, nor did she turn to the luminous landscape filled with a dense light that in the past had always brought joy to Raymonde's soul, for she recognized this light in real landscapes or in paintings, Anna, inflexible and glacial, didn't turn her rigid brow to these landscapes, this land, it was as if she were already absent from her body, and for the first time Raymonde, her mother, must confront the prospect of mourning, yes, of the desolation Raymonde had talked about one day to Guislaine, adding that the vision she had had of Anna at that moment could be compared, she felt, with that of an angel afflicted by some hidden rot, as if in Anna's gaze, in her hands intertwined on her knees, under the sinister fold of her lips, there was some latent decomposition that threatened to surface, to grow, while other girls her age were savouring this summer day, abandoning themselves to it absentmindedly, even as their mothers looked on. Suddenly, for Raymonde, the blue sky that could be seen from the window, the summer harvest, all these landscapes that she loved, that she had awaited for years, hoping to offer them to her daughter, on that day the sky was eaten away by Anna's illness, by the poisonous substance of her anguish, yes, on that day Raymonde had lost Anna, perhaps forever, and the beauty of the landscape she had so long felt nostalgic for had in turn been fissured, bruised, Raymonde had confided this sorrow, this desolation to Guislaine, her friend, whom she did not tell everything, for a subtle class difference had come between them in college, Raymonde a child of the bourgeoisie, Guislaine a poor scholarship student who came first in class, with her noble profile, first everywhere, yes, but wasn't failure etched on Guislaine all the same, as it was now on Michelle, was she not haunted by all the doubts that disturbed her daughter, but one mustn't betray oneself in their presence, instead feign courage, insolence, especially with Liliane, already so insolent and several heads taller than her mother, tell oneself that while Liliane's forehead was touching some mysterious zenith she, Guislaine, was shrinking, bowing down with the years, towards the ground, but no, that wasn't true, not so soon, no, "Mama, so beautiful, so sexy," Michelle said, giving her no peace, pestering her, importuning her with her affection – when she was affectionate, for it wasn't every day – and now these sticky fingers on her new books she hadn't even had time to open, in the corner of the house she had had the temerity to call her domain, Michelle's acrid, alcoholic odour, that fetid presence still hovering in the air of her room, lamenting her fate, "Mama, Mama, you don't love me, you don't love me enough," and hadn't the dark source of the illness been revealed by Michelle, yes, by Michelle herself, and the transparent intuition that was her nature, without a psychiatrist's help, because there was some tattered secret she shared only with Michelle, in an intimacy both of them found frightening, which they never mentioned though both were victims of it, Michelle was right, Guislaine didn't love her, didn't love her enough, Guislaine, Paul, hadn't wanted Michelle in their life, Liliane, yes, their joy at the birth of the first child, above all the hope of enduring longer, through Liliane, of being reborn, and the strange witness who was suddenly there, whom they called Liliane, who was singularly ambiguous, she would not help them extend their days but, rather, might reduce them, dangerously, with all the unease, the worries she provoked. In the past, long ago, they had cooed in her ear, Liliane, our chubby little sweetheart, our very own baby, Liliane examining her parents, their folly, ironi- cally, she wouldn't be possessed like that, they weren't going to conquer her with their gifts, the material indecency they were so proud of, no, that gigantic sparkling presence in their lives had suddenly embarrassed them, and yet they had loved her, Liliane, they were still students and looked at the chubby imp who jumped into their bed in the morning, her jam-stained hands soiling the books they were studying, gradually they became resigned to it, telling themselves, she's very healthy, that's a blessing, look at her pink cheeks, her bright eyes, she understands everything so quickly, she won't be a difficult child, but Michelle, Michelle was an accident, Guislaine hadn't been careful or they'd had too much to drink that winter night, after a long day's skiing, Michelle probably knew, guided by her unfathomable lucidity that warned her of all dangers, all disasters, that her parents – especially her mother, only her mother was guilty of that – had conceived her one winter night without loving her, negligently, already rejecting her, utterly distracted, forgetting this life, Michelle, this irresolute life that was suspended among them, that was already moaning in the winter silence, you don't love me, you don't love me enough, this tattered secret that she shared with Michelle, she had entrusted it to Raymonde, only to her, but Anna wasn't like Michelle, a life, you had to dare to say it, to think it, an embryonic, accidental life such as you see on the road, accidents, the dead, lives lost through forgetfulness, utter absentmindedness, Anna would be Raymonde's sister, her friend, Anna would be loved, desired, even from the depths of her chilly abyss, Raymonde would never be resigned to this loss, this abandonment, one day she would give her daughter proof of her love, Raymonde would never say, like Guislaine, my daughter is wrong, no, she would say don't you see, it's the world that's bad, the pure essence of Anna's life, Raymonde would say, is what I want to defend, and Liliane was thinking, as she held her ecology petition, of the hordes of foxes, of deer that were abandoning the country, the forest, for the outskirts of cities, drifting, drifting around our frontiers, in our garbage, for the hunters had uprooted them and slowly they were heading for collective death, with no more strength to struggle, they would come to die in our midst, to beg for a final, abject peace in our own abjection, ferreting about among us, in our rubbish, these hordes of foxes, of deer that we had already massacred,

Michelle, Liliane thought, Michelle would never see them running in their woods, their forests, they had already been killed by men, when Michelle realized, later, just how illusory was the pleasure afforded by drugs, where would they be, the hordes of foxes, of deer, and the stags that were killed every day in Scotland, in the zones of our abjection already piled high with our cadavers, she, Liliane, would save the planet, Michelle, my little sister who has to live, Guislaine and Michelle were going out together, Guislaine's hand was touching Michelle's arm, they resembled one another, Liliane thought, they formed a radiant couple of women, of girls, who pleased her, her gaze, her feelings, her nature, Liliane seemed to be approaching them to kiss them, her mother gently pushed her aside exclaiming, "Heavens, you're tall, be careful, we're more fragile than you," and Liliane began to talk of a nocturnal trip across an icy lake, not the canoe trip, which she seemed to have forgotten, Guislaine thought with relief, but one night when the three of them had gone out together, fleeing for a few hours their grandparents' country property, one Christmas night, "We saw a dozen deer go past in the woods," said Liliane, "and it was your idea to walk across the frozen lake, it was crackling, remember, we could feel the water starting to flow underneath," Guislaine pushed Liliane away, saying she'd never been so crazy, so madly foolish as to take her young daughters out on a barely frozen lake at night, and Michelle told Liliane that she remembered the night, they had made snow angels, lying with arms outstretched and hollowing out their shapes in the snow, in the morning, in the sun, the shape of our outstretched bodies was still there, Michelle smiled as she recalled it, in the snow, in the sun, their shadows melted, Liliane's vast silhouette towered over hers, "Really, I'd never have done that, I'm a responsible mother," said Guislaine, but Michelle's dreamy smile reassured her, as the temperature had dropped sharply that night, she remembered, hadn't Guislaine been certain the lake was frozen, the distant muffled sound of cracking under the patina of ice hadn't worried her, but it was like the canoe adrift in the night, she felt she was suddenly caught in a trap, in the middle of her daughters, that violent crackings were colliding under the thin ice, that soon they would be reproaching her for the tumult of these troubled waters that never reached the point of freezing or of massive inertia, as she might have wished, the distant muffled sounds of cracking could no longer be ignored, they were so near, their echoes resounded inside us, kept us from sleeping, she thought, beneath the apparently frozen surface there were smouldering fires, and that was the main reason why Liliane and Michelle reproached her, for having cast them adrift in a canoe, in the middle of a calm night that would become, before dawn, a night filled with fierce and vicious storms, no, she must forget these sinister images, these bad dreams, Liliane was simply nostalgic for a world that was still a welcoming place for the animals and all who dwelt on this earth, the hordes of deer, of foxes, was it not nature's degraded innocence that offended her most, and Guislaine listened to Liliane, thinking, I'm the one who feels persecuted, it's not reasonable, why should they take so much pleasure in attacking me, torturing me mentally, they aren't cruel, after all, I know them well, they're my daughters, I've watched them grow up, things aren't so bad between us, and the old lady was asking her son, in an irritated tone, what they were doing there, stopped on the bridge, while a hundred motorists were blowing their horns around them. "We're waiting for the traffic to stop, Mother," said Paul, he was looking at the woman who was his mother and telling himself, I must be patient and fair, "You'll be home soon, Mother," he said, curbing his anger, once again on this same day a woman was molesting him, irritating him, Guislaine, Michelle, Liliane and now his mother, he looked at her cross face beneath its crown of freshly set and tinted hair, the dry lips that were still muttering, scathing words still fell from them, sounds that seemed to repudiate him, expel him into the solitude of a father without a son – "Yes, you pay dearly for those daughters of yours, and what happiness do they bring you? My poor child, if only they were like other girls, but what bad luck, heavens above, what bad luck, I don't dare invite them to visit me on Sunday any more, as I used to, and do you know why, son? Because they're simply not presentable," his mother had said nothing, Paul thought, he could read these thoughts on her face but she had said nothing, she would be late, she said, but there was no one waiting for her now, aside from her teeth, which were giving her trouble, hadn't her doctor recently told her that her health was excellent, that she could live a long time yet, on her way home from the hairdresser she had bought a new lamp to brighten up her living room, she was holding it on her lap now, under a pile of boxes, looking straight ahead, thinking that she should have told her doctor, but why live so long, there are already too many fossils like me on this earth, she despised their pity, their disdainful exchanges, they didn't love her enough, she could read under this lamp, as she watched passersby on the street, the hours would be long and she always got up too early, very often at the same time as her cat, no, things were no longer as they had been in her husband's time, Liliane, Michelle had grandparents then, they could be pampered at Christmas, surprised with kisses on New Year's Day, sweet and mischievous, they were their mother's pride, their grandmother's, "You know, Paul, now that your father's gone the days seem very long," she confessed to her son, but his suppressed hostility suddenly made her not want to confess anything more, and the words only flickered on her lips, they were still motionless on the bridge, horns were blowing around them, the bridge vibrating, dense and hot, Paul thought, while a muffled rumbling ran through his veins, was he going crazy here in this car, so close to his mother that he seemed to feel her breath on his neck, but his mother, her face turning purple in the heat, was saying nothing, she held her lamp on her knees, expressing a great deal of reticence at being there, beside her son, which astonished him, that was it, perhaps, the reticence she had always expressed in his presence, a sort of reticence that was perhaps how she felt deep down, in life, with him or with others, as if she were secretly threatened wherever she went, he told himself that such feelings were exaggerated because they were related, mother and son, and this tie suddenly seemed to him grotesque, incestuous, as if her reserve were welding them together in a single absence of love that had, with time, become incestuous, for he was so accustomed to seeing his mother, before or after the hairdresser, the day she went to see the dentist or the doctor, watering his plants when Guislaine was away, taking care of his daughters when they were little and had measles, that he could no longer imagine life without her, nor she without him, perhaps, "But that lamp's much too big for your little living room, Mother," he said, looking contrite, the old lady, flattered by his remark, looked affectionately at Paul, if he mentioned the lamp she'd bought, it must mean he sometimes thought of her, of her monotonous suburban existence, so he didn't completely forget about her, he was a good son in spite of everything, she'd never found fault with him, and he was still the boy she'd always known, but he read too many abstract books, wrote too many abstract things himself, perhaps he didn't really write but only reflected what others thought, there was too much moral pressure on university professors, just because they read a lot they weren't necessarily creative, he had married so young, "Why all this commotion?" she asked, the trucks, the cars on the bridge, how hysterically they all behaved to fill the hours that seemed so long to her, endless at times, and then the untidy young hitch-hikers with long hair, terrible things would happen to them too, Michelle, Liliane, raped, molested, pushed into a ravine in Mexico or elsewhere, that was what came of education nowadays, of the loosening of morals, for a long time now, like their parents, they hadn't been going to church, the old lady looked at her son, a university professor, an intellectual, she thought with contempt, Paul was right, his mother was reticent and her reticence was complete, absolute, there was a truly cross face beneath the crown of freshly set and tinted hair, the face of a mother telling her son, "Stop bothering me, I'd rather live without you, without them, you don't love me, you don't love me enough."

"Let's go out for dinner, just you and me," Guislaine had said as she led Michelle away from Liliane, towards the stairs and then onto the street under the hot, heavy sky, calling her "my little girl," and now they were eating, facing one another, in a luxurious hotel restaurant where students played Vivaldi during dinner, "You could be playing in an orchestra like that soon," Guislaine said to Michelle, but Michelle was taciturn and looked at the pink salmon, the potatoes intact on her plate, "Why aren't you eating?" Guislaine asked, exasperated, "You're clean and pretty tonight, why aren't you eating like everybody else, if you'd only tell me why," Liliane had bathed Michelle, what right did she have to dispense such nourishing tenderness, what right did she have, Guislaine thought, to bathe Michelle? "I thought you enjoyed coming here, because of the music," said Guislaine. "I do like coming here," said Michelle, food was desecrated when millions of children had perished in Biafra, Michelle listened to her mother, watched her, and squirmed with embarrassment on her chair, Michelle could hear in her lungs the breathing of silent agony, in Biafra or somewhere else, she didn't have enough air, her heart, her chest bursting in one final respiration, "Why aren't you eating?" her mother asked to the sound of the flute, the oboe, the piano, she was dying under her mother's eyes, those eyes whose gaze she liked to draw to herself, it came at you from so far away, from under those voluminous lids with the long lashes, so far away. "Remember that nice friend of yours who used to accompany you sometimes on the violin, whatever became of him?" "Nothing, Mama, he's nothing, still nothing, he hangs around the streets, that's all," Michelle seemed to say, shrugging at her mother, and Guislaine longed for a house filled with children, with laughter and music, which she'd never had, for she was at the hospital from morning to night, constantly absorbed by a life that was not her own. Guislaine had finished eating, the skeleton of a chicken languished in a brown sauce, "Come on, eat, what's wrong with you, the salmon's fresh and pink, the colour of your complexion when you're healthy." "But I'm not healthy now," said Michelle. "Of course you are, you're healthy but you're behaving like a rude little girl tonight!" "Liliane says salmon are dying by the thousands in our rivers." "Oh, don't listen to everything your sister says, anyway your sister's not like other people, you shouldn't listen to her all the time." "Mama, you're so beautiful, so sexy." If Michelle didn't pour these absurd compliments on her mother as she often did in public, Guislaine thought, it meant she wasn't feeling well. "Darling, eat just a little," she said, holding a bit of potato on her fork towards Michelle's mouth, but she had scarcely started the gesture when she was suddenly filled with disgust at the thought of Michelle's sticky fingers soiling the pages of her diary, of her books, in the one room people were forbidden to enter, she withdrew her hand and with it the offering of food that Michelle would have swallowed, but only with her help, at that moment, for she seemed to hear a desperate cry from Michelle who was suddenly alone, adrift in the canoe, or here across from her, Michelle's heart, her chest would burst, perhaps, but she wasn't sobbing, she wasn't weeping, she wept dry tears, that was it, Michelle thought, dry tears, the day before, even today, she'd thought she would faint in the street, hadn't she had that vision as she was walking, it was shortly after leaving Anna, the air was as red as Anna's T-shirt, a red stain on the horizon, Anna was setting off on her bicycle in the suffocating air, the air tightened around you, heart and chest pounded convulsively in one last breath, you saw the skeleton, the small bones already melted, you saw the heart palpitate one last time, making a tremendous effort, under the fleshless black skin of the children of Biafra, and now Michelle was feeling that silent agony, they were all dying with her, through her, and her parents were dying too, and Liliane, and the young people who were playing Vivaldi as others ate and digested their meals, and outside the vultures were waiting, watching, soaring above their heads, the vultures were the only ones who didn't die, thought Michelle, the vision, Michelle's vision, her hallucination was clear, she was going home as usual, very late, her music books under her arm, and she realized that they had all been annihilated by fire – her parents, Liliane and thousands like them – the house, the furniture hadn't been broken or damaged but under the fire-reddened sky all the people had been given up to the silent flames, each one had been pulverized, taken by surprise, the red bodies of her parents were there, and the fire-reddened body of Liliane as well, and thousands of others all around now, standing or lying, under the thin covering of their fire-reddened skin, and Michelle wept dry tears, tears that smelled of fire, that were quick to dry. "But what's wrong with you, why aren't you hungry?" asked Guislaine. "Once your periods start it will be different, look at your sister, she's always hungry, but you shouldn't have drank your father's gin, that was probably Liliane's fault." "It's never Liliane's fault," Michelle wanted to protest, but she said nothing, Guislaine heard Michelle's cry, this startled breath of hers, but she was powerless, she thought, powerless, the canoe was adrift, she no longer held it back, it was like the time Michelle had pneumonia when she was three, they could hear her coughing in the dark, whole days, whole nights, Guislaine, Paul, her dry tears, tears that didn't flow, they heard her muffled lamentation in the dark, what are we going to do, they all gathered around her bed, looked at her eyes widened by fever, "You'd be warmer in woollen socks," on one side Paul, on the other Guislaine, each of them warming with their hands one of Michelle's feet encased in a white woollen sock, each one listening, hearing the torrent of dry tears that no longer flowed.

The woman who came from Asbestos broke the vast expanse of water, of sky, she thought, she dared to approach Alexandre who was reading in the sun, or writing, she leaned towards him, looking at his hairy cheeks, his hair blowing in the wind, not a young man, she thought, an animal, but there are a lot like him nowadays, and she dared to say to him, "Rita, my name's Rita, I'm telling you because you asked me my first name," and Alexandre smiled, bent over his book again, he left his tent-flaps open on rainy days so Marc and Pierre could take shelter, and every day he brought them a supply of hotdogs because that was all they'd eat, which disconcerted him somewhat, when he was here, thought Rita, the children never went to sleep on an empty stomach, yes, she had broken the vast expanse of water, of sky, she had dared to approach him, and now she was look-ing at that sky, that sea devoid of hope, catching a glimpse of her sons' legs in the distance, in the waves, spindly legs and arms she must soon clothe in their cousins' rough overalls, they wouldn't go to school this year, they would just hang around in the city or on the beach, still she must go through the motions of dressing them as if for school, would she go on washing dishes in the fishermen's tavern, they were all so base, or would she take her children and go and live with the truckdriver who had offered to take them in, all so base, what was the good of drowning her days, her nights, in the steamy tavern that reeked of alcohol, wouldn't she become an alcoholic like her husband in such a setting, she was already taking a drink in the morning because he had gone, she'd never been in the habit, it was get-ting late in the season, life was dull, bland, with them or with-out them, soon the fog would come, the cold, hadn't Alexandre reprimanded her because one day she'd absentmindedly pinched Pierre's ear, she would have liked to punish him even more, to bite him in her desolation, beat him, it wasn't that seri-ous because Pierre's skin wasn't sensitive like Marc's, why had Alexandre gone away, if he was selfish like the others, still he had a charitable soul, he always came to the defence of the weak, he wouldn't let anyone be humiliated in his presence, hadn't he told the woman from Asbestos that he was prepared to die for that idea, which seemed insane to her, it was easy to see all that writing was disturbing his mind, you couldn't prevent someone else's humiliation, she had told him, "It's all that writing you do day and night, it's disturbing your mind," heavy white birds, starving, were standing everywhere, the beach would soon be deserted, and she had confided to Alexandre the indomitable, courageous name of Rita, Rita who is nothing, Rita and her children who have been thrown out in the street.

Anna had shut herself in her room, she wouldn't go out again, thought Raymonde, or perhaps this time it was just a temporary crisis, but Anna's bicycle was padlocked to the garage door in the yard so she must have decided not to go out for a while, it must not happen, thought Raymonde, it mustn't, this can't be happening to her, Anna's dog, which she'd again forgotten to take out, was scampering behind Raymonde in the yard, and Raymonde thought of the meeting that would be held tonight at her house, more Security Centres, more prisons they would say, how could you prevent it when they knew now that the girls were just as fearsome, tough and unyielding as male delinquents of their age, and as numerous, they no longer knew where to house these girls, pimps, pushers, and they could kill too, a pair of fifteen-year-old delinquent girls had stolen a car and run over a woman and left her lying on the street dying, and they had described this murder without regret, like some casual event, how could they be allowed to live like that, among other young people, stirring up mutinies in schools, colleges, Anna's island, her compressed space, her animals, the parrots that flew freely through the kitchen, everywhere this catastrophic disorder, more Security Centres they would say, more maximum-security prisons, pushers, pimps, thieves, murderers, and Anna's imprisonment had begun long ago, thought Raymonde, instigated by those very people who thought they were protecting her, yes, they themselves had made the decision with all its ramifications, with their ideas about reform, the educators, the sexologists who recognized only one form of sexuality, condemning any exceptions as society would have done, everyone who worked with her at the Institute, reform Anna by killing her, it wasn't dark yet, why had she already switched on the lamp in her room, more Security Centres, more motels where they would spend their weekends under a surveillance that seemed lax yet was enforced by police, even at rest they would be under surveillance, and Michelle who had thought she could be part of those groups, those gangs of savage tigers, no doubt to get closer to Anna, they were all the same, the watchers and the watched, Anna had been imprisoned so long ago now, even when she came back from Florida, from the Caribbean, she had never left her headland. Anna was gazing at the wall her mother had once painted pink, she saw Tommy, Manon go past, mingling with a black funeral procession; they, who had no respect for white civilities, were joining their destiny as a mortal couple with the person who lay there, isolated and compact beneath an iron lid, in this procession, all the faces were smiling, offering up to the already incandescent air the flashing of whites of eyes in dark faces, the dazzle of immaculate teeth in the light, only Tommy and Manon, who were following the ceremonial at a sober, deferential pace, were not smiling, they were dull and silent beneath the brilliant colours they wore and it seemed, Anna thought, as if they were suddenly attached to these hours, this life they had disdained, not understanding it but suddenly alerted, by the wing of decomposition that buzzed through the air, to the fact that the dead person's soul, revived now by these joyous faces, the music of these dancing bodies, was pushing the iron lid aside, seizing the sprays of flowers and scattering them and itself across the landscape under the blazing bright blue sky, exclaiming, "I have been delivered, now I am free of all your ills, I will disperse myself like pollen, spread myself through the fluidity of air, sky, water," and yet, Anna thought, they should have understood at that moment, as she herself understood, the meaning of this fleeting journey they had undertaken, always so near the frontiers of death, for they carried with them the exultation of that journey, and its end. Just the day before, they had indulged in prostitution together in a single eccentric embrace, this time without perfidy, going to a hotel with a rich, degenerate old woman, who said as she kissed each one in turn that she would ask nothing of them but a little of their youth, and to merge for a moment with their ecstasy, their lustful games, that was all she hoped for, yes, to fasten her gaze, which would soon be extinguished, on the savage, energetic beauty of their youth. They, the outlaws, thought Anna, had consented, without calculation, without vice, who knows, refusing the money they were offered if such was their wanton whim that night, they had consented to the sharing, or to the gift of decrepitude, because that image of old age had first moved them, won them over, under the arthritic fingers that smoothed the crow's feathers they wore on their heads on festive nights, so much, thought Anna, that in the stinking mazes where their hunger led them, they often maintained, as their heads rose above the gulf, the dignity of birds of prey. They had felt her fingers shuddering under their tangled hair, pressing avidly against their sunburned skin, those hands, those arms, and suddenly they recognized the shudder of an old forgotten love, if they could still arouse desire weren't they estimable, why were they being driven back to the ruins of the earth, Tommy, Manon moved past on the wall once painted pink, they paraded by in a black procession, dull, silent, sometimes at the corner of a street, when they raised their heads to the sky, their faces seemed livid against the sparkling day, Anna was walking quite close to them, discreetly effacing herself, panting, her skin gleaming with sweat under her ragged Indian tunic, like all the objects she had touched with Tommy, Manon, shredded by wear, panting, there would be a meeting at the house tonight, her mother had told her, she thought she could hear Raymonde's footsteps outside, Raymonde, her dog running among the trees and bushes in the yard, so far away, with her bicycle padlocked to the garage door,

on the far side of her island, so far away, but the deaf stubborn-
ness of their lives, of their footsteps appalled her, diminished her
silence, the majesty of her silent visions on the wall, they were all
there, longing to be noticed, heard, they would come tonight to
hold discussions with Raymonde around the table, therapists,
educators, she would listen to them, impassive, rigorous, more
Centres should be opened, more prisons, Rehabilitation Schools,
but outside the cities this time, in zones surrounded by barbed
wire, and far from the cities, out in the fields, they would be invisible out there, underground lodgings for Tommy and Manon,
thought Anna, the Correctional Institute wasn't strict enough,
the girls knocked down walls with axes, they were allowed to go
out on weekends, escorted by their parents, but they escaped too,
they were never entrusted with a key, they were constantly spied
on in their rooms, in the corridors, they had no keys, not for
going out or for coming in, hostile, warlike, a race of slaughter-
ers, these children tore the leather from armchairs with their scis-
sors, ripped open mattresses, trampled books from the library,
every object entrusted to their symptomatic barbarism, they
would say around the table – and Raymonde would listen to
them in silence, thinking of Anna in her room, on her island,
thinking of Anna's existence, reclusive, self-effacing, "You have
woven a sash of oppression, of suffocation, around them," she
would say suddenly, but she would utter the words in vain, Anna
was motionless, gazing at the wall once painted pink, Peter was
lifting Sylvie in his arms in an attitude of devotion and love, as
he still held Anna in his arms, Anna, so small and already tough,
beneath the crimson California sky, Sylvie, shaken by her father's
strength, laughed her crystalline laughter under the crimson sky,
it was like a cascade of weeping, of sobbing that tore Anna's
heart, "It's nothing, you're alive, that's all," he said; "When we're
learning how to live, the growth of our first teeth, our first hairs

causes us pain," she heard Peter's breathing in the evening breeze, in the water's roar, it was elsewhere, later, that he and his imperious voice would enter Anna's world, that delicate and supple world of young dancers, suddenly admiring her reticent grace during a ballet class, he would run his hand along her stiff leg bound in silky white tights, obstructed by her tutu, she could feel, all along her leg, his invasive gesture that made her blush before her classmates, Peter, Dad, I hate you, "It's nothing," he said, "Why are you looking at me like that, I'm just admiring a step, a movement," or else he said nothing, only looked deep into Anna's eyes with that monstrous, infinite tenderness that so soon, Anna thought, would die, would cease to exist, "Why aren't you eating?" Guislaine asked Michelle, "You must eat," they had a vocabulary she didn't know, perhaps she should ask abruptly, "How much coke did you snort today in the toilet, what pushers did you run into at the disco, that's why you're always blowing your nose," but Michelle's nose was hardly red, no, she didn't snort coke, how vulgar and unpleasant those expressions were, that vocabulary, how repugnant, she would not let herself be debased like so many other mothers by that language, that depraved alchemy, Michelle didn't blow her nose any more than usual, you knew Liliane had affairs with women, her smell was powerful, sensual, at least you could imagine anything about Liliane, but how could Michelle's sickly habits be detected from her angelic profile, perhaps she was blowing her nose a little more than usual, maybe she'd caught cold on her way back from the swimming pool, "Listen, eat, stop tormenting me, a little dessert at least, don't you want to make me happy?" "I love you Mama, you're so beautiful, so sexy, I like going out with you, you know, I enjoy the Vivaldi, but I'm not hungry tonight." "So beautiful, so sexy," Guislaine replied impatiently. "Stop saying that, it's ridiculous, that's no way to talk to your mother, where were you and Anna this afternoon?" Guislaine went on. "In a park, Mama," Michelle replied, submissive, to the sounds of the flute, the oboe, Michelle was wasting away as her mother looked on. "In a park with bums, exactly, I've told you to stop associating with those people, they have lice, you'll get them too." "It's been a long time since I've lent them my bed," said Michelle, "They'd rather sleep outside in the summer." Guislaine imagined Liliane bathing her sister, cajoling her, rocking her, it was an occupation unworthy of an older sister, who knows, perhaps she'd been taking a bath with a girlfriend, that professor of sculpture she always talked about with such ardour, in the folds of water, a bath, a swimming race, when Liliane first tasted sensual pleasure on the lips of another woman, a timid contact, no, she didn't want to know about it, when Liliane washed Michelle's hair did she pick away the lice, Guislaine didn't have the courage to do that, to lavish all these considerations on Michelle, Guislaine would have liked to cry, to howl at the sounds of the flute, the oboe, good Lord I'm unfair, she thought, so unfair. "You must eat," she said gently, touching Michelle's cheek, and suddenly her entire being began to tremble, under her voluminous eyelids with their long lashes Michelle saw her mother's eyes fill with tears. "Mama, you're so beautiful, so sexy, and I'm upsetting you," but Guislaine was already sobbing uncontrollably, "I can't bear it," she thought, "I can't bear it," the tears flowed and flowed, down her lightly made-up cheeks, onto her silk scarf, the canoe was adrift, she thought, under the black spruce trees, in this spacious restaurant where they were playing Vivaldi, Michelle got up, went over and took her mother in her arms, sitting close to Guislaine on the same narrow chair, she said nothing, her eyes were dry and burning, her heart was pounding wildly, Michelle's sticky fingers, purified, refreshed by her bath, gathered up the tears that flowed down her mother's cheeks, silently, with painful propriety.

The fog had been so intense for some days that Rita wondered, wasn't there a danger its fibres would suffocate you? Day and night the lighthouse sent out a long, lugubrious moan that sent shivers through the woman from Asbestos, her solitude as an exile, a wanderer, was released by this strident, doleful moaning, the summer now drawing to an end had seemed long to her, full of people who hadn't understood her misfortunes, one single person, among all those lying on the beach or prowling through the town overheated by air and sea salt, just one soul had approached her in solidarity, Alexandre, but then he had fled like the others, to the Pacific or somewhere else, always farther, his pack on his back, his hat pulled down over his eyes, and it was only to him that she had confided her name, the baggage of her broken life whose pieces, she thought, were worth no more now than her wedding dishes, they had all fled, abandoning the town with its closed shutters and silent fog-chilled streets to those like the woman from Asbestos who were only passing through, adrift, swallowed up in their own unechoing silence, only a few days of dazzling sun were left, tribes of summer visitors were tossing their carefree cries into the air, Rita had caught a glimpse of them when she went to fetch her sons on the beach strewn with their garbage, their indecent repose, her myopic eyes behind thick glasses had cast angry, indignant glances at all of them, sometimes with a contained appeal, but it had touched only one person, Alexandre, and already, even as she looked everywhere for him, as she was looking for her son Pierre who had wandered off, she thought, in the opaque wave of fog, who knows, perhaps she wouldn't find him, "Pierre, where's Pierre, Mama?" asked Marc, buried in his coat, blocking his mother's steps. "Don't get on my nerves, you know he's always disappearing but then we always find him, don't worry, I see a lighted sign over there, we'll stop and ask where he is, after all the village isn't that big, these fishing villages are always small, you could be a fisherman, later, if we stay here." They had been walking for several hours already and Marc was clinging to his mother's dress, complaining that he'd eaten nothing but a hot-dog since morning, "Some days are like that," said the woman from Asbestos, "other days are better, I've some crackers in my bag if you want, can you hear the foghorn? That's to guide the fishermen when there's fog or a storm, life has good days and bad days, you must be patient," but Rita knew Marc had reason to complain, if it weren't for the Portuguese truckdriver who gave them lodging wouldn't they be out in the street, where was Pierre, once again she had pinched his ear in a fit of temper, was it her fault, Pierre was always irritating her, but the man who gave them shelter was despicable because he had beaten Pierre, Pierre who was not his son, she hadn't protested, or hardly, for some time now she'd put up with everything, from exhaustion; they'd been walking for several hours now and she could smell the fetid vapour from the tavern that clung to her clothing, her glasses, misted over by fog, hid the greyish sky and sea from her, over there, against the row of wooden houses with drawn shut-ters, they would stop and have a coffee soon, she told Marc, who kept asking for his brother, "Anyway," said Rita, "even if he wanted to get a job as a cabin boy, who'd want him, eh? This damned fog seeps right into your bones, we must be the only people outside on a day like this," and she laid her hands on Marc's skinny shoulders thinking, how much longer will he last, he's dissolving, but a boy's coarse laughter suddenly cut through the air, it was a gangling black boy who was laughing as he skipped along the other side of the street, you could barely see him but in the fog his gait seemed demented, he laughed, skipped, he seemed to be wearing an old soldier's uniform which he'd shortened himself; it hung from him, from his lunatic gait and his hysterical laugh, in this fog that diminished every sound, like the incarnation of a vagrant madness, dislocated and alone, no doubt, were his laughter, his gait crucified on a violent past, wondered the woman from Asbestos, it was that memory with its disconnected images that skipped along with the boy, who knows what explosions of unspeakable terrors he was delivering himself from in this way, with his casual movements, laughing and crying at the same time in the fog, "You never know what might happen to people, remember that when you grow up," said Rita, taking her son's hand, and he asked again in a quavering voice, "Pierre, where's Pierre, Mama?" "Over there," she replied, "in the tavern that's always open, you know he often goes there, he thinks we won't find him but we always do, now stop getting me all worked up over Pierre," but Rita's heart was humiliated by her certainty, Pierre had been beaten for a trifle, even she could no longer remember why, she hadn't defended him, she had taken part, for the first time, in an offence she considered to be grave.

And a few days ago, she thought, it was summer, and she came to these dunes, these beaches and looked at this blue sky that inspired only thoughts of suicide in her, but there was no order, no wisdom in those thoughts, you had to choose life over nothingness without hesitation, the blue sky did not soothe her; sometimes, without knowing why, she smiled at the cloudless sky, at the fine sand under her feet, feet sheathed in shoes which she compared to the shoes of nurses or nuns, what was she doing here in her ragged flowered dress, encumbered by a destiny that was aimless and, above all, bereft of any sense of order, what was she doing here amid these naked, shameless bodies gilded by the sun, perfumed and oiled, she looked out at Marc and Pierre on the horizon, they, so sickly, didn't belong to this race of gods and goddesses, she thought, basking in their beds of sand, of water, beneath an untroubled sky, they were only Marc and Pierre, children without a father now, children dressed in their cousins' overalls, children whose mother had no work permit, in a foreign land, but despite all that, when she thought about it carefully, she preferred life to nothingness, they shouted with delight, leaping in the waves among the other children, Rita mixed with no one, sitting on a sand hill or standing, her dress blowing in the wind, she remained isolated; a group of young women was laughing, chatting or reading as they offered their bare backs to the sun, from her hill of sand, off to the side, Rita sometimes dared to sit down and stretch out her legs in their coarse beige stockings, gazing at the tips of her shoes, thinking, with all these people undressed around me I wonder why I don't take off the boys' overalls, but their underwear is too badly worn, naked, they have pimples on their bottoms, I really can't let other people see those, let them enjoy themselves, they'll forget their drunken father and how poor we are because of him, Rita had had to sell her wedding dishes, sell Marc's toys too, but she hadn't hesitated, you had to choose life over nothingness, hadn't Alexandre given them a ball they played with in the waves, a Portuguese truckdriver had taken them in, no, it was better not to complain too much about her fate, some superb horses and riders were travelling over the dunes, the naked young women were being watched under this guileless blue sky, in these pleasant spots where the rituals of male constraint seemed to have been abolished, a bare breast, a thigh was identified by a distant rider, on the dunes, and the image he retained in his binoculars – of a woman's body he had briefly violated from this lazy retreat where he remained, reared up on his horse – made him swell with reckless sensuality, and the pleasure he felt, on his horse, extended his authority from the nipple he had moistened with his eye's caress, as a filthy fly might have done, to the nuclear installations being erected with the power of his sex, his cunning, overconfident power, gigantic and incalculable above the thousands of lives, ephemeral as dragonflies, teeming between sky and water, ignorant of the approaching fire that burns and sacrifices, who would have thought, tanning them- selves in the sun by the undulating sand and water, who would have thought of the horsemen of death out there on the dunes? Rita, from her hill of sand, heard the steps, the muffled neigh- ing behind her, they were indeed the horsemen of death, she thought, rending the air with their factories of destruction, but the young women laughing and chatting seemed to notice nothing, Rita wished she could lose herself in their ranks but she was looking at the tips of her shoes, observing with myopic eyes behind glasses a young woman wearing an old-fashioned white bathing suit, and very pale beneath her suit, she too might be called Rita, thought the woman from Asbestos, for she too was unable to join the other women, she was without friends, with- out companions, she had left behind her, like heavy burdens, a tearful little girl, an obese husband, and the sandwiches they were unwrapping on a blanket, these acts she had seen so many times, and so many times submitted to, on vacation, the tearful little girl, the obese husband who's always hungry despite his size, she turned away from the two of them sitting heavily, ready to eat, pale and white, the whiteness of youth already somewhat drained of colour by sullenness, she tried to approach the laugh- ing, emancipated women, there it is, in their midst, she seemed to think, my freedom's homeland, close by she heard the little girl crying, but no, they were still sitting heavily on their blanket, the obese man, the sniffling child, and suddenly, seeing all the women so radiant and emancipated in the sun, the open air, she lost her courage and stopped walking, but rather crawled through the sand, thinking that way she would pass unnoticed, and Rita saw the pale figure crawling under the sky towards that far-off and inaccessible recognition of friendship, crawling towards the other women, she would be able to talk about everything, and be understood, all pale in her white bathing suit, her white face, shamefully hopeful, lit up at times by the flash of a smile, but the smile was a fold of sorrow, the other women were sleeping, reading on the beach, those who liked to swim walked past her, loosening their hair in the wind, she was there, her name might be Rita too, naked as the day she was born, her terrified body in the old-fashioned white bathing suit, she was crawling slowly in the sand, the other women didn't see her, didn't hear her, she was barely visible, she only knew that in the trembling of the air, the water, these heavenly and inaccessible eyes, arms, lips were saying to her, "Come, come closer to us, we'll console you for that fold of sorrow that has replaced your smile, you who think yourself invisible when your whole life is throbbing so close to ours, come, come closer to us."

From the hill of sand where she was sitting or standing, at those rare moments when she took advantage of the sea air, beneath the lumpy mass of all the bathers, the woman who came from Asbestos also saw – sometimes a white form like the woman in the old-fashioned bathing suit, as the tall waves came closer weren't they silently preparing to immerse her, to swallow her up, for she would return to the obese man, the little girl, she wouldn't leave them; sometimes a woman draped in a frayed silk fichu, who sat under a parasol all day just a few steps from the woman from Asbestos, massive and dignified; in that position she saw these forms, in the distance or quite close to her, thinking that perhaps the statue's face might turn towards her, just once, and talk to her, expressing, in the labyrinth of her wrinkles, of her impassive resignation, a grimace of goodness, for there was goodness, Rita thought, on that face which seemed to say nothing, express nothing except some sort of harmonious passivity lived and assumed without too much rigour, what struck Rita, next to that statuesque passivity, was a man, the sedentary husband who had organized this trip, transplanting to this place his house, his crossword puzzles, his case of icy beer, and among these domestic objects of his, the parasol and his wife, impassive objects in his eyes, because his reddening flesh, the colour of raw meat, Rita thought, was roasting in the sun from morning till night, he never talked to his wife or looked at her, it was as if he possessed but one domain – himself, the sanctuary of all that sunbaked flesh, at times his gaze beamed with lust when he looked at the other women, but it didn't linger elsewhere for long, on the texture of those brown or pink skins that were unknown to him, soon the fat grey man would cover himself lavishly with lotion and cream, he thought himself handsome, those arms, those hands and their velvet covering of grey hair, and under the hair on his chest was that mass of reddening flesh like raw meat, his life was so comforting that he saw neither sky nor sea, only the wall of flesh that wasn't crumbling, the resistance of those muscles that weren't breaking down, at times he would look tenderly at his gaping bathing trunks, shouldn't one admire such an ardent quest for one's own pleasure, Rità thought, at these difficult times, and at such moments she considered that, even if the blue sky often filled her only with thoughts of suicide, perhaps the woman draped in her mauve silk fichu was right, and the imperious Narcissus at her side, smiling amid his overflowing flesh the colour of raw meat, celebrating with his sedentary, earthbound body his obsequious cult of the self, and then existence, existence, perhaps it was only that, a woman whose statue's face no longer saw him, no longer heard him grunt or moan with pleasure, the wife of this astonishing Narcissus was voluptuous too, perhaps she danced at night with the young fishermen from the village, secretly preserving her subtle dreams when her husband's dreams seemed too concrete to her, these dreams emanated from him, drooling and greedy, welling from his gaping trunks, from the hair on his belly, as if he were saying, let someone caress me, love, me, no one can do it as well as I, I love myself so much, no one could love me more, the man's flesh diffused, his wife's too, and drifted in the air, Rita thought, drifted with its perfumes, its milky odours, its sap, its contented exhalations, and old Narcissus was delighted by it all; as long as the mounted policemen on the dunes don't see me, thought Rita; they'd send me home, and Rita suddenly had a vision of Asbestos, of a silent collapse, of the men she'd never see again disappearing into the mine, there would be an earth-slide, with no crash or roar, and the little school with the slanting roof would perish in an avalanche of mud.

"You can have crackers and coffee as soon as we stop," Rita told her son in the fog, his agility was disturbing as he followed his mother, from time to time she touched his temples, his damp hair, "and a hamburger if you're still hungry," he was there in the folds of her coat, her dress, so light, she thought, the humidity made their faces wet, seeped into their bones, hadn't the summer fled since the Portuguese truckdriver took them in, once again it was the same life of toil, of worry, and the weight of that man who had taken pity on her, too, they had had the illusion of travelling, of going away, and suddenly they were moving laboriously through the icy fog, and the thought of the truckdriver was still there in Rita's soul, how many times had she had to send the children outside, in the middle of the night, for the satisfaction of his desires, their desires, they'll go and play the slot machines, the pinball machines, said the man, chasing them away, the children had a mattress on the ground, the man and Rita a bed, the bed was there, guilty, blackened by all the abomination on earth, she thought, she had a lover, she who considered herself unworthy of being loved, she had had a husband, a drunkard, all the same she would have preferred not to cheat on him, even though he used to beat her when he was drunk, but now the order was broken down, living meant having some sense of order, she could no longer tell herself, everything's in order for today, the laundry is on the clothesline, the boys' socks darned, we're poor but decent, the immutable order of her existence had been betrayed and now there would be only chaos, she had left Asbestos carrying heavy parcels, now she suddenly had nothing, no property, no possession that might have justified the pain or anxiety of her existence, but no, she still held in her hands one agile bundle, Marc – her entire property, still safe and warm, "I won't lose you, you know, and as for Pierre, we'll soon see him again, out of the corner of our eyes, wearing his baseball cap, drinking a Coca Cola, he'll have found someone to look after him, he's always telling tall tales, a real martyr if you listen to him." "And you're going to ask him to forgive you," said Marc. "You're crazy, you listened to that Alexandre too much, you too; don't forget that people like him, people who write things all day long, don't forget that their heads are mixed up, the most important thing is to have your head in order, even when you've got troubles." But the Portuguese truckdriver's bed was still there, with lumbering shadows under the sheets, she had to tell them to play outside, even at night, at their age she had a duty to protect their virtue even if she had lost her own, and at the pinball machines the big boys were smoking joints and trying out harder drugs where they would find the poetry of life, the serene, transitory detachment that she had felt, briefly, when she looked at the sky, the sea; this disorder, this wreck of their lives merged with the colour of the water, of the sky, suddenly grey, the sky, the water, or perhaps the poetry of life, the joy that had brightened her days concealed only suffering, she thought, Rita was a realistic woman, first she must find Pierre, improve her life with her sons, but anyway, gradually, one day order and decency would return, someday they would have a home, a shelter that would endure. The truckdriver's bed evoked for her that blazing summer day when no one could be seen in town, Rita was looking for work, walking through the blazing, hostile town, her sons at her side, she remembered that day well for she had pinched Pierre's ear and in a fit of temper Pierre had told her, "You'll be sorry when I go away for good," shouldn't they learn to be tough, like men, their hollow cheeks, shadows under their eyes already, but that was in Asbestos, here things would be different, life would be less degrading, they were walking near the harbour and in an abandoned shack a couple was making love, beneath the baking sun that heralded a storm, on this street where no one came except for a few dogs that prowled around looking for food under the doors, the windows slowly being weakened by destruction, crumbling, the couple making love in a tattered armchair reminded her of the Portuguese truckdriver, his guilty bed filled with the corrosion of life, she too – the woman from Asbestos – was flotsam in the sun, in the light that dazzled her, blinded her, she saw once more the slow-moving couple and their corrosive laziness in the sun, he was young with a blond mane, he hadn't taken off his jeans, you couldn't see her, and the slow decor that accompanied them in their descent to the very heart of the heat, the exhaustion of this airless day, their sweat, like Rita's, ran slowly, in exasperation, the truckdriver's bed was a stopping-place on the edge of time, the putrefaction in the abandoned shack at noon, the inert couple, and in the armchairs the final sentinels were noble dogs, strays, starving but lucid, who observed this decadent superior race, the race of man, that was no longer redeemed by the motions of love.

Anna was gazing at the wall that Raymonde had once painted pink, Tommy, Manon were moving away with their black procession, soon they would disappear at a bend in the street, she wouldn't see them any more, not at night or at dawn, she could hear her mother's footsteps outside, her dog running, come back, come back, they all said, that insular life is dangerous, you lose your senses, lose hope, your appetite for life, her return and her solitude began in Miami, obeying an unknown pusher in the airport, Philippe, who was waiting for her, her or another girl, but whose face was still unknown to her – it would not be someone else but her, Anna – locked in the toilet she had thought mockingly, that strange man knows nothing about me, I'll be afraid for him, I'll give him my courage, vindictive and proud, who could reduce Anna's strength, touch her chilly mind, and she felt fear, a sealed and silent fear, none of them would ever know what fear she'd felt, it was time to return, a time for solitude, and suddenly there was Philippe, Philippe who would need Anna, need her fear, and she would place in his slender hands untouched good – a drug that heals, lulls, exalts; she would lie at his side, it would be an island again, Tommy, Manon, a journey without end, always identical to the one that had gone before, because you desired nothing more, good, evil and their supreme mockery, thought Anna, every moment lived only to be lost, the neutrality of all that, the void, absence, wasn't Anna's one savage passion her desire for such neutrality that any feeling of pain would henceforth be cleansed, expelled from her heart, and yet those hours of her life were replayed on the wall that Raymonde had once painted pink, the sickly faces of Tommy, Manon faded from sight at a bend in the street, in the black funeral procession, to the echo of a mortuary celebration that was not sinister but filled with laughter and song, Tommy and Manon were going away, alone; at the Miami airport Anna had decided to continue the journey, proud, vindictive, and that was how an older man saw her coming towards him, you wouldn't say here is Anna coming back to her mother and her dog and her birds, her return would be muted, a second disappearance, but this time nothing would be known of it, Tommy said you had to shoot up so you didn't feel anything, the airport had suddenly seemed like a place that would protect her vertigo, she walked slowly through the turbulent crowd, a transparency within her, and within them a similar transparency, the designs on her Indian tunic were transparent too, like glass foliage, this tunic she had washed the day before, like her hair, but the odour of the sun, the hot perfumes of the earth were still there, on the straight ends of her hair, and there she found the intoxication, the perfumes once more, she walked cautiously, afraid of stumbling, for her body was aching under the Indian tunic, the trial of patience she was submitting it to – her body, which had known only languor, inertia, must be stiff and tortured under this trial, this display, the flight would be long, she thought, but she was surrounded by luminous façades, outside it was still summer, when the man called Philippe, who lived in a skyscraper, fell in love, at his window, as if with a sign of hope in that silent landscape, with the snow sparkling on the river, where would Anna find that divine drought, the drought that had burned his thoughts, his torments – a hallucination, a trip, thought Anna, would create nothing but brief, concise, always identical expectations, she was already overwhelmed by the tempestuous crowd, a tiny African child had around his neck a placard on which was written, in black letters against his yellowish shirt, Number 2, it was as if this solemnly garbed child, who looked more like a work of African art than a child, Anna thought, was one of the ancient princes of his race, left behind on a leather seat, on the shores of our continent, from a work of art admired in a museum, he passed from prince to what we had made of him – Number 2 – Anna looked for a long time at the young king adrift in the airport, whom aristocratic black parents would come and fetch, but who was suddenly, for Anna, only a number like so many others in the swelling crowd, she should, thought Anna, have taken him to her headland, to her inlet, where, incorruptible and upright, he would have kept intact his lineage and his name, but parents covered in gold and jewels, dream parents created by the imagination of whites, would hoist Number 2 onto their shoulders and she would never see him again, tomorrow, later, who knows if Number 2 might not instead be like Tommy's brother who swept the steps of escalators when they were stopped at dawn, a sweeper as Tommy too was in danger of becoming, Anna thought, an orange turban wrapped around his head, tired, already very tired, like the young sweeper, who was neither prince nor king but a Number 2 who had emerged from his bronze mask, a banal reality like so many others in the white world, thought Anna. Suddenly, in the airplane, her fear sealed within her, she knew she was sweating with fear, and who knows, perhaps they all knew, those who were close to her, comfortable, forgetful of the fear they themselves might have felt, because the fire, the lightning of their death preceded them everywhere, under the wings of an airplane, everywhere, but they rejected this doleful evidence of life and death by their relaxed attitude, they took off their shoes, stretched out their legs, and Anna's soul shuddered with fear, from now on her journey, she thought, or the transparency she had felt during her journey, would be alert, watchful, wasn't she like Tommy, Manon, during their expeditions, they too had dreaded this trance of fear, but what was there to be afraid of just now, she was sitting beside a boy of about twelve and his mother, they smiled confidently at her, the mother, accustomed to her strange son who played with dolls, opened her newspaper, smiled at Anna, while her son took out his dolls, the work of a miniaturist, the dolls lay in a nest of cotton wool in a small box, the boy had made a whole collection of dresses, coats and jackets for his dolls, from a variety of fabrics, Anna felt calmer as she looked at these products created by innocence, an innocence she had lost, had furiously deprived herself of when she was the boy's age, so as to confront the others who were her enemies, those who ruled the world, her fiercest enemies, like Sylvie, laughing and playing by the swimming pool, this boy still had the quality of his independence, he was creative, his imagination would be delirious, if tomorrow he were allowed to live his fingers might draw, paint, thought Anna, his mother respected his vocation for such a peaceful art, without constraints, he would have plenty of time to read the newspaper she was reading now, to hear the rumours of war, and she smiled at Anna as she smiled at her son, her generous smile welcoming them into this torn world where for centuries, she thought, even at times of cholera or plague, artists had survived, where everyone had learned to survive, she seemed to be telling Anna, but Anna felt like crying, it was too late, she thought, she no longer played innocent games, she was entranced with fear, and she was afraid for this woman, this boy, more than for herself, Raymonde who had never given up hope for Anna, ever since her birth, now she would probably have told her, "You see, Anna, you too can come out of your inertia, don't you understand that you'll soon be back with us?" and suddenly she fell again into those sly traps of the earth, those who spoke of destroying the universe, Anna thought, would the customs officer allow them through like dignitaries, receiving servile bows, Anna wondered, no one persecuted these merchants of mourning and death at the borders, but Anna, Tommy, Manon were followed to the frontiers of these countries, everywhere they dared go, but they were forewarned, circumspect, even Anna who had washed her hair before leaving, the custom officers, male and female, were waiting for Anna as if she were their prey, she thought, though she suddenly pretended to be like that image of Anna Raymonde would have liked to see when she returned, even if all about the straight ends of Anna's hair there still drifted those summer smells, forbidden aromas she wanted to turn over to Philippe, she knew she wouldn't listen to the man when he told her, "That poison's not for you," but it was late and Anna was back on earth and a charming, inoffensive young customs officer was talking to her as she opened Anna's bag, she asked Anna to remove all her personal belongings and Anna obeyed as Tommy had taught her to do, to feign obedience, foolishness, just the way they liked to see you, and Anna told herself that she resembled Raymonde, or the image of Anna that Raymonde liked to see, they wouldn't see who Anna was underneath, Anna was tough, vindictive, they would know nothing about that, what had Anna been doing all this time, travelling, yes, but Anna was so young, she had been studying far away, where was her diploma, the young woman and Anna looked at each other with mutual sympathy and without knowing it Anna, like Tommy, Manon, was the victim of an investigation, a persecution, the official's strategy escaped Anna, who suddenly observed the young woman reading, with apparently sympathetic interest, the notebooks she carried in her travelling bag, Anna's words, written under the influence of drugs, were now printed in the air, with all their obscure, impenetrable signs, Anna's inner life was there, however, on these pages that a power-hungry customs offer was trying to decipher, but Anna compared her obscure signs, even when they were subjected to pressure from the system, to the rigid writing in Indian temples, impenetrable, she thought, impenetrable, no one could tell if her thirst was for water or death, for rain or annihilation, the gods had already rejected her, and Anna's body was aching, she was afraid of being stripped bare but she would betray none of her pain, tough and vindictive, she thought, let them search me, probe me, I am Anna, impenetrable, as well as her shampoo hadn't she decked herself out with red lips, painted nails, a clean tunic with faded designs over white jeans, who knows, perhaps an ordinary girl, the customs officer seemed to think, shrugging, or else it was true, she was the daughter of rich people and had gone abroad to study, the customs officer bit her lips, she didn't like Anna, Anna who had been studying abroad, but how pleasant it was, suddenly, thought the customs officer, to be the judge, the one who hands down the sentence, to be all that and be a woman, these faces, these gazes were there before you, filled with uncertainty, at first she had obeyed her superiors, then, seeing how feeble their authority was, she was becoming the soldier in this place without men, and looking at her Anna thought, you could understand how treason could spring up in isolation, in women's souls, for treason was perhaps above all a voracious feeling of jealousy, the customs officer didn't like Anna, Anna who was rich and studied abroad, Anna wouldn't be a pusher to be put away in a lugubrious prison from which she would never return, the customs officer, whose duty it was to surprise, to punish, to put people away, reproached her for travelling to further her education, while she herself stayed behind watching departures, arrivals until she grew weary, in her blue uniform – like the navy blue worn by airline hostesses, but her own monotonous, routine life was riveted to the ground here, Anna was talking with the toughness of her intelligence, the coldness of her wit, about her father, an American dancer with a famous company, he was a choreographer, he was often invited abroad, the customs officer listened to her, biting her lips, with increasing hostility, cruelty, she thought, is also the vice of the simple, however she wouldn't give in this time, thought the customs officers, this girl seemed formidable, perhaps she was, she knew the words to defend herself, to attack, "You young people," said the customs officer, who wasn't thirty herself, "you don't like us, to show you that we aren't so terrible, you won't be searched." That was her proud victory, thought Anna, over an invincible prey, others would be punished in her place, Anna had been the sort of prey she dreamed of, the customs officer was sorry to let her go, thought Anna, and thinking of Philippe, of whom Anna knew nothing more than his name, his address – she would learn later that his parents, his grandparents had died in the Second World War, for several months Anna would be Philippe's only family, his reason for living, he would tell her, later; thinking of Philippe with whom she would reach her journey's goal, thought Anna, she told herself it was this spitefulness or easy cruelty of the customs officer, which had so often shocked Raymonde at the Correctional Institute, that maintained an irrepressible force in this world, for this unhealthy force that men exerted among themselves, in their armies, their dictatorships, had been passed on to women as they exercised their lesser powers, and the victims of these women were often other women, Raymonde had said, that's the way, thought Anna, under the gaze of a female customs officer who was a party to masculine cruelty, that other women would suffer after her, the act of denunciation, of punishment, yet in the unambiguous young face that had smiled at Anna there had been, at first, only a sympathy close to tenderness, Anna thought of Philippe whom she did not know, she had returned to the world of man where past and future merged into a single *idée fixe*, the degradation of the human soul, "You see, there's no reason to be afraid of us," the young customs officer was saying, but Anna knew she had come back to a human story in which tears would flow, endless, bitter and violent, and torturers, informers were always there, pleasant, smiling, affable, she knew, too, that if she was back in their midst it was to take part in their crimes.

Michelle and Guislaine were walking under the hot evening sky, languid from the wine, Guislaine wrapped her right arm around Michelle's frail shoulders, after all this fierce heat the storm would be welcome, she said, "What a beautiful night and how short the summer is, but this winter, you'll see, we'll go skiing, I won't leave you again," Michelle listened to her mother, Guislaine stroked her cheeks with her fingertips as Liliane would have done, Guislaine never rested, summer or winter, thought Michelle, she never had time to rest, why was she telling these happy lies, these dreams, "We'll hear the sound of our steps on the snow," said Guislaine, "and you'll be healthy all the time." "That's nice, Mama, but it isn't true." "Of course it's true." "You know very well that it isn't, it's just dreams," said Michelle, kindly, "Do you want me to tell you a dream I had? Liliane was by my bed, I was asleep and she woke me every hour to kiss me, she held me very tight in her arms, she'd kiss me and then I'd go right back to sleep." "That's not a nice dream," Guislaine observed; "Obviously your sister's kisses are still very ingenuous, but I think it's indiscreet to look at a sleeping face, she doesn't know, she can't be aware of it yet, you understand, despite her size she's still a child, we know that, her parents, and your black curls spread over the pillow, wouldn't that awaken her sensuality, she's already so advanced for her age," Guislaine murmured to herself, "What do you think, Michelle?" "I don't know, Mama, wait, I want to tell you about another dream, you had knit two wings for me, of blue and gold wool, I think, they were spread open on the lawn like the wings of a miraculous butterfly, but I didn't dare try them, though I dreamed about flying as high as the trees, like Anna on her bicycle on the air, the fire," thought Michelle. "Why didn't you dare?" Guislaine asked suddenly, "They're your wings. Don't tell anyone else about this dream, they might distort it and it wouldn't be yours any more," they looked at one another pensively, silently, they walked more slowly, "I love you, you know," Michelle said softly, "even though you're hateful sometimes," it had been a long time, thought Guislaine, since she'd seen Raymonde alone, wide wings on the freshly cut grass they could no longer use, thought Guislaine, Michelle's dream was simplistic but touching, everything about Michelle was like that, had that form, that breath, she was simplistic, touching, sometimes ridiculous, her child, when they still saw one another it had to do with this single tortured exchange – their daughters, Anna, Michelle, Liliane, who were they, Anna, Michelle, Liliane, what would become of them, their voices were silent, their little secrets in suspense, the women could distinguish on one another's brow, under their eyes veiled by insomnia, marks, wrinkles on their passionate and youthful faces, that was it, thought Guislaine, they still had so much passion for life, Anna, Michelle, Liliane, weren't they riddling their mothers' lives with all their latent problems, and Guislaine thought of the dying – boys and girls now familiar to her, whose diseases had no remission, no child should die, it was amoral that this fact, this deterioration had to be hidden from parents, from friends, but you saw them in the newspapers at Easter, at New Year's, a clown, a clown so kindly visiting the rows of beds, amusing the waning lives, the emaciated, hairless heads, Guislaine took Michelle by the waist, as yesterday she had put her arm around Raymonde under the trees in the college yard, "You must eat," she said bluntly, suddenly, "yes, how do you expect us to keep you alive if you don't eat?" Michelle made no reply, thinking of the album in which she noted all the suicides that concerned her; she wondered how one young suicide victim, among others, could suddenly decide to live, not die, her name was Janet, her friend John lay dying under a tree, near Mount Hannah, his wrists slashed; nearby was a spring; someone flying over the mountain in a helicopter had found John's body against the tree, Michelle thought, victim of the drug "paraphernalia," a cure, who knows, a calming intoxication, John had shed his blood in the solitary night and later, under the first rays of dawn, and yet a spring, the source of life, was nearby, why hadn't he wet his face there, quenched his thirst, during a final feast beneath the implacable light of the sky, seeing all the blood shed in vain when the source of life was there, so close, generous and abundant, Janet had fled, thought Michelle, she would have liked to take on her shoulders the diaphanous burden that was John, her friend, brother, lover, to tell them all, "I saved him from the drug paraphernalia, wash the blood from his wrists," but resolving to live was a selfish act, no one had time to look back, John would always be there, under a tree amid that ecstatic arrangement of flowers, of sunbeams, supremely reconciled with all he had loved, nature, his innocence, the purity of his love for Janet, soon he would be dissolved, forgotten, yet he would always be there, haunting the spirit of Janet who had fled in that sublime, selfish choice of survival – survival that thinks only of itself, that's afraid, that cries even as it runs – he would always be there, too, in the thoughts of Michelle who opened her album of souvenirs every night, an album of horrors her father called it, yet it was so real, the only way to forget nothing, thought Michelle, was to look everything in the face, with no help from parents, psychiatrists, for they would all rather ignore the dramas in this album of horrors, and Guislaine told Michelle, walking more slowly now, gentle and pensive, "I'd like to read that book about Cosima Wagner you were reading, when I have a little time, perhaps this winter, why not, this winter when we go out of town, when I take some holidays with you and Liliane, your father too if he wants," if Michelle passed her examinations, next year she could enter a class in composition, she thought of the fugue she would compose, everyone wrote the same kind of fugues, restrained and classical, she thought, but Michelle could write a Wagnerian fugue in which she would recount all the confusion of her life, her fever, her anxiety, her dry tears would be as resonant as bells, people wouldn't say, "It's just like any other fugue," but "What rough and gleaming chaos, melding with the sound of bells is the echo of bombs and the cries of those whose tears have been burned away," they exchanged a look of complicity, "You know, what Paul says is true, Guislaine, I'm not developed enough yet to take the pill," "Your father's a man, he can't know everything, look, there's going to be a storm, you can feel it in the air," and their heads, already close together, touched as they walked. "You told me your dream, thank you, it's rare, I could have hurt you by my reaction." "But it's different with you," said Michelle, "you're my mother." "Why is it so different, do you think I'm better than the others because of that?" In the past, thought Guislaine, she went out with Raymonde, went to concerts with her, now they saw one another so seldom, Michelle wrapped her frail arms about her mother's shoulders, she murmured very quickly, "That wrinkle on your forehead, I know it's there because of me," and Guislaine made no reply. Anna was gazing at the wall her mother had once painted pink, she heard Raymonde's footsteps outside, her agile, deliberate tread, her dog panting as it ran under the trees, all that was happening so far away, on the other side of Anna's island, she remembered Sylvie's first drawing, which Peter had shown her with pride, a drawing of a thin black cloud in the sky and, under the sky, caricatures of Peter and Sylvie sleeping on the green grass, Peter lifted Sylvie in his arms, put her down on the grass saying, "Come, angel, we're going to learn how to walk," and suddenly a thin black cloud formed in the sky, as in Sylvie's drawing, thought Anna, Peter wondered, why is there a cloud in the sky on such a fine day, he looked at his swimming pool, under the sky, and his new little girl at his feet, and on the sunny terrace over there, his new wife who would soon serve drinks in opalescent glasses, no, he must dispel the notion of that cloud in the sky, Sylvie stretched out her arms towards the mild and luminous world and Peter said, "Be careful, angel, you mustn't fall, you're already dizzy, don't be afraid, I'm right here beside you," dizziness, he called it, the thrill of feeling all this beauty around you, the water, the light, the fluidity of the air, dizziness, he said, it was a restorative thrill but it would drain your strength, he said, wasn't Sylvie, suddenly very weak, afraid of falling? Peter's anxious eyes were watching the advance towards Sylvie, who was playing and gurgling at his feet, of the thin black cloud, that ball of poisoned gas that snuffed out all life in two minutes, a thin black cloud in Sylvie's drawing, her first, which he had shown to Anna, so proud, so happy to share with Anna the first expression of Sylvie's spirit, a drawing, its ingenuousness, and that thing was coming imperceptibly closer, an ink stain, thought Anna, against the pale sun, the woman on the terrace, Peter, Anna fell to the grass without a sound, one after the other, a light ball of poison gas that snuffed out all life in two minutes, Peter, his wife, their little girl didn't get up again, perhaps they had fainted, in a vast unrebellious silence, yet Sylvie's heart had stopped beating, the lime trees were covered with coarse black dust, the roses were already dead, and drop by drop the thin black cloud was seeping into the blue water of the swimming pool, Anna thought, Peter had not foreseen this black cloud in the summer sky, on this marvellous day when he was helping Sylvie take her first steps, the exhilaration of life, of existence, of being, of rushing towards our first deliverance, to breathe, to walk alone, Peter, the conscientious objector, had always told Anna, "Your father will never kill," he who thought of everything had neglected to anticipate this scene, "I, Peter, will never kill," he had said to Anna, to Raymonde, while examples of barbarism marked all his days, all the hours he lived with Raymonde and Anna, ate up his happiness with Raymonde and Anna, conscientious objector, he got up one day, his garden destroyed, a child in his arms who was no longer breathing, a thin black cloud in the sky as in Sylvie's drawing, a gas that snuffed out all life in two minutes, his life, Anna's life, Sylvie's life, in two minutes, Peter had imagined fire, ashes, the scattering of mutilated bodies, he had forgotten the existence of that thin black cloud in the sky, Sylvie's foreboding, so concrete; nature's last resources, the last survivors would be dotted along the beaches of Honfleur, in the Boudin reproduction that Raymonde had put up on the wall for Anna, Anna's life was scarcely breathing, she too was touched by the thin black cloud advancing peacefully towards the earth, slowly, soundlessly, in a great silence, and in a few moments it would snuff out everything that lived.

Lying in the grass, hands folded under her head, Liliane was looking at the sky which heralded a storm, she would sleep outside tonight, in this meditative position, the far-off rumbling of thunder didn't frighten her, at dawn she would go fishing, alone, often alone, taking her boat out to the middle of the river, one day she would bring Michelle here, under a starry sky, some hot summer night, or under a troubled sky like this one a few days before autumn, they would cross the river side by side in the same tranquil, fraternal motion, Guislaine would no longer say, "Liliane will kill herself swimming back and forth across the river without stopping, you mustn't go with her, Michelle, it's dangerous," Guislaine would not be there, motionless at the riverside, expressing her fears, her anger when they swam out of sight, away from her protection, "You're both crazy, come back," Liliane would take her mother down to the calm, shady river, she would lead her by the hand, with a gesture of confidence, sometimes she came here with a privileged girlfriend and they slept entwined on the grass, Liliane waking up from time to time to observe her friend's features in the beam of her flashlight, the night shed light on her face, her pure features that would change so quickly, under the thick hair that she pushed away with her fingers as if she were asking this forehead, these cheeks on which no fateful signs had yet been inscribed, "Who will you be tomorrow? Will we still be healthy, free, as we are today? Will you be able to defend your ideas, defend me too, if I need it?" The fire that Liliane had lit glowed in the night, every now and then she tossed twigs on it, watching the sparks that collected by the short grass at the river's edge, "Being alone like this is almost as sweet as being with someone," she murmured in the night, lying gently on the grass; she was thinking too about the ecology meeting she had attended tonight, her friends were right to say that if the heads of state were prophesying an era of deprivation, such deprivation would be an ordeal not for them but for others, for didn't they live in an extreme and insolent luxury that provoked rioting among those they oppressed and kept under their yoke, didn't all that virile hypocrisy have to be denounced, Liliane got to her feet, I am tall, huge, monstrously strong, she thought, reflecting on these attributes ascribed to her by her parents, she got to her feet, stirred up her fire, she was tall, majestic, stirring her fire under the sky, who were these distinguished impostors who loved luxury, money, power, did they care about the life of Anna, of Liliane, did they have the slightest concern even in their own homes, within the bosoms of their families, or had deceit blinded them past the point of plausibility, until they were unaware of their own annihilation? These young lives who heard their treacherous words every day, thought Liliane, knew that they never told the truth, that even in their tolerance they were false and deceitful, they forgot that in the schools, colleges, in the streets, fragile shields were being raised up everywhere, these shields were words, already, tonight, in a disused room in the college, these words denounced and struck, they said, "Beginning today, we must learn how to survive," but who would these people be who had the leisure to survive, already humanity could not live decently, those who talked about surviving were not the wretched and the poor, but those who already lived abundantly, who were buying, selling, what they quite shamelessly called "survival food," yes, thought Liliane, they would be tomorrow's survivors, not Michelle or Anna, she thought, but those who were stocking their cellars not just with grain, with dry, sterilized food, but with guns to kill their brothers, tomorrow, thought Liliane, to survive would be another form of repression, of revenge, in which the weak, the poor, the wretched would be conquered in a massacre that would not even be deemed scandalous, these shields – words – were rising up everywhere, in the schools, the streets, and one day they would have to be listened to, North America would have its atomic shelters, in India they would perish by the thousands, thought Liliane, that was the justice of today's society in which she lived, the superficial smiles you saw everywhere, on television, in the newspapers, the burlesque faces with so little connection to the responsibility of living, Liliane and her friends no longer wanted to see them, to hear their voices announcing the end of the world without a quiver, when we were still in the Middle Ages in our thinking, in our outwardly civilized and polished actions, the fire glowed in the night, Liliane dived into the river that all day had been warmed by the sun, she swam close to the shore, never leaving the circle cast by her fire in the night, its sparks shooting into the glimmers from the sky, it was still a beautiful summer night, Liliane would swim for a long time, she would return here often by herself, in autumn, in winter, mulling over this question, her future, their future, how many lethal images in that word – future – but others long before her had confronted the murders of history, the woman who taught her sculpture, who was European, had told her those heroic names, Rosa Luxemburg, Käthe Kollwitz and many others whose existence she had until then been unaware of, and suddenly the boundaries expanded, Guislaine's and Paul's house where she had armed herself for her first battles was like her little sailboat on the water, wavering in the night winds, she must swim towards the open sea, guide them all towards the marvels she had discovered, why had she doubted her strength, since all she wanted, for herself, for all of them, was happiness, permanent and indestructible happiness, dignity for every man and woman, how many revelations life had offered her, so young, the sensuality of love, of friendship, didn't she feel that sensual veneration for her mother when she kissed her every morning before leaving the house, placing her lips on that painful wrinkle under the beautiful hair on her brow, "I hope you'll change in time," and Liliane thought, even if Guislaine repeats that sentence every day I, Liliane, will not change, "Yes, you must change," Guislaine pleaded, but Liliane thought no, no Guislaine, you have time to subdue all your fears, but I will not change, she would come to this same fire in winter with an athletic friend, they would cook, join hands over the fire under the pale winter sky, the wan sun reflected on the snow, both of them moved by the inexhaustible vitality that united them, transported each towards the other, they were rising up, these words, these shields, everywhere, thought Liliane, refusing the time of deprivation for some, the time of death for others, in the past women had written in prison, no rule had enslaved them, they had written, I am alive, I resist, I will not give in, no hunger strike could break them, could break into the song of their will, their vitality, thought Liliane, nature was being depopulated and the animals, decimated, were heading for suicide, the words were crying out on all sides, "The wolves, the whales, these species you are sacrificing will not forgive you for your crimes, tomorrow your gardens, your forests will be deserts of ashes, sterile valleys without leaves or flowers, the plaintive animal will come here to die in your pools of blood," Liliane's teacher had talked to her of the heroic names, a few women among the rest, and she thought, I too, Liliane, will manage to confront the murderers of our time, and returning to the shore where her fire was glowing in the night she spent a long time bending over her broad, powerful hands, peering at their form and their lines, she would be as strong as an oak, yes, she would be able to write, sculpt and love with tenderness, live without servility, she had been taught that under Stalin's terror a Russian woman had survived torture for a long time by reciting a poem by Pushkin to herself every day, survival for Liliane, tomorrow, in who knows what Nordic hell, submitting to torture for her ideas, her principles, perhaps she too would struggle to survive by reciting the words of a poet, the prayer of a mystic, what she knew deep down was that with her broad powerful hands she would sustain the lives of others, as a Lesbian artist she had already known in her own family life the blind rush of discrimination which was also that of society's courts, which tore children from their mothers for a question of sexual preference, in Dallas or here, lives could be crushed, Stalin's terror was not an event from the past, tomorrow, to survive with her mother, her sister, a friend, Liliane might perhaps have to recite to herself – during a hunger strike, during the torture of deprivation and cold – the words of a poet, the prayer of a mystic, while imprisoned in some Nordic hell, her bright pink blood freezing in her veins.

For several days now, thought the woman who came from Asbestos, the fog had been oozing from the walls, the houses with their closed shutters, chasing away swimmers, tourists, the long moan from the lighthouse piercing the silence, at times footsteps, voices, their plaintive, grieving sounds swelled the moan from the lighthouse, like the coarse laughter of the black boy who was skipping through the streets, the entreaty from the depths of adversity that Rita now no longer feared, for she herself had become that entreaty vainly extended through the silence of the universe, everyone had left, thought Rita, but some newcomers wandered through the chilly fog, like the woman from Asbestos, they came in groups, they came from nearby towns to see the ocean, and their pilgrimage was airtight and peaceable, didn't they prefer benign invisibility under layers of fog to blue sky, the sharp sparkling of light on their sores, buses arrived during the days, the weeks, when a persistent, almost nocturnal fog prevailed around Rita, malevolently streaked with pink at sunset, these buses, these cars released a crowd of people and their teachers, some suffered from cerebral palsy, and like the giggling boy they had a swaying gait, arms of different lengths, and nothing seemed to connect their movement to the hidden balance of their bodies, they walked together, strained their ears, listening to the sound of the waves, the moan of the lighthouse, day and night, others suffered from mongolism, all of them were virtually children, thought Rita, perhaps it was their custom, and the custom of their teachers in specialized, painfree homes, to take them out during this season when an uninhabited, fogbound city was transformed into a graveyard, but as in graveyards where grass and flowers grow, a place where life still germinated, humid vegetation in the fog, in fields already transfixed by the approaching cold, an irresistible life, a life in waiting, that men, the living, no longer threatened, for in this world, thought Rita, only the dead were respected, they came like wild animals leaving their dens, sniffing the water, the air and the cold, dense fog that embraced their bent limbs, breathing into them, along with the invigorating sea salt, their precarious resurrection which for a long time now human love had no longer given them. The fog oozed from walls, from houses with closed shutters, evening was approaching, night was already filtering the rose-coloured radiance, unexpected in the fog, soon it would be night, Marc was still there, huddled, warm, thought Rita, in the folds of her coat, "I bet you he's there, in that tavern," she said to her son, "in that seedy tavern where Alexandre often used to offer him food, if I know your brother he'll be there," and as she opened the door of the tavern Rita saw Pierre sitting at a table with some drunks, not drinking but sipping a Coca Cola, and he wore his cap over the corner of his eye, as she had imagined when they were walking through the fog, he was there and he irritated her once more with his wasted face and the circles under his eyes, an old couple who hadn't left the tavern for several days now, an old woman, an old man who seemed to have no complaints about their fate, thought Rita, chewing on their chunks of bread, their dry crackers like the ones Rita carried in a brown bag on the road, a frail paper bag, the crackers crumbled, thought Rita, she looked at the grimacing smiles that greeted her, and among them her son Pierre who did not smile at her, it was this wasted face with the circles under the eyes that had told Alexandre, "I'm going away with you," this face that would never cease to trouble Alexandre's soul, when he had thought he would go so far away, to the mistreated Aboriginals of Australia, to the Zonards in Paris who slept on the grilles of the Metro in winter and ate from restaurant garbage cans at dawn, those Aborigines, those Zonards were so close to him that he would always see Pierre's wasted face, his eyes ringed by hunger and despair, Pierre's hand clutching his while a voice in the fog pleaded, "Don't leave me, don't leave me, I'll be beaten," Rita looked at the child she had brought into the world, "Come on, son," she said, "we'll continue on our way, we haven't reached the end of the road," he looked at her suspiciously, she was his mother, Marc was his brother, he decided to get up and follow them.

The last resources of the earth, the last survivors were dotted along the Boudin reproduction, thought Anna, on the wall Raymonde had once painted pink, we will never again see all that water, all that light, she thought, only in pictures, that water, that light, a painting will contain our convalescent visions of another life, another century, tomorrow, when we finally seek the cure for all our ills under the impression of our society's agony, our collective agony, Tommy and Manon were moving away in their black procession, and Philippe, of whom nothing remained but a sweat-stained garment on a chair, they were all going away to leave Anna to her visions that were ending on a wall, absentmindedly she stroked the head of her dog, felt the rush of her birds whirling around her in the room; it was time for the meeting, they were sitting around the table, the ones who would open more Security Centres, more prisons, from her room, her island, she heard those sincere, honest voices that desired only Anna's annihilation, there would be new reforms, a crackdown on laws that dealt ruthlessly with minors, Raymonde was saying nothing, listening to these voices, saying nothing, sitting erect at the end of the table, austere, silent, she looked at these dispensers of justice, saying nothing, Anna's visions were ending, Philippe was opening his arms, saying to his captive child, "Go away, you must go away, the shape of your head could be embedded forever in the hollow of my shoulder, and in the captivity of my love you'd be stripped of all your rights without knowing it, go away Anna," and she descended the stairs, the steps of that limbo they had known together, sweetly inseparable, she was going towards the roads of her cold conscience, thinking of Tommy, Manon, their ineptitude for living, her own, at the edge of grottoes, of islands, all that was left of Philippe was a sweat-stained garment on a chair, already one man in this wretched world had suffered, had loved, because of Anna, and in her greed, Anna's greed, she had consented to leave him, choosing, over love and happiness, the roads of her cold conscience that would lead her nowhere, she thought; thus Alexandre had wrenched himself away from the comfort of Raymonde's rough love, thought Anna, when he would not hesitate to throw all his notes on Dostoevsky into the wind before an innocent, unjustly punished face, perhaps, Anna thought, Alexandre had reached that headland, that inlet, where Tommy and Manon prowled in the ravines, crawling through garbage beneath a sky soon to be blackened by the ashes of destruction, from that headland, that inlet, the confines of Anna's despair, perhaps the hope, the thought of return might touch him, for one day the visions on the wall would end, thought Anna, we chose to die or to return, they were all there around the table, and Anna heard their voices, the sounds that were hostile to her youth, to her life, Raymonde suddenly told them all that she needed to rest, to reflect, "a long year to reflect," she told them, and they listened gravely to her around the table, Anna opened her bedroom door, she was leaving her island, Raymonde came up to her, not daring to believe it, she thought as she held Anna against her heart, I think this time she's come back.

Related Reading

Dey, Claudia. *Stunt*.
   Toronto: Coach House Books, 2008.

Erpenbeck, Jenny. *The Book of Words*. Trans. Susan Bernofsky.
   New York: New Directions, 2007.

Foad, Lisa. *The Night Is A Mouth*.
   Toronto: Exile Editions, 2008.

Irigaray, Luce. *Speculum of the Other Woman*.
   New York: Cornell University Press, 1985.

Jaeggy, Fleur. *Sweet Days of Discipline*. Trans. Tim Parks.
   New York: New Directions Publishing Corporation, 1993.

Lewis, Paula Gilbert, ed. *Traditionalism, Nationalism, and Feminism: Women Writers in Québec*.
   Westport: Greenwood Press 1985.

Lispector, Clarice. *Near to the Wild Heart*.
   New York: New Directions Publishing Corporation, 1990.

Marks, Elaine, ed. *New French Feminisms*.
   New York: Pantheon, 1987.

Rigney, Barbara H. *Madness and Sexual Politics in the Feminist Novel; Studies in Bronte, Woolf, Lessing, and Atwood*.
   Madison: University of Wisconsin Press, 1978.

Sellers, Susan. *The Helene Cixous Reader*.
   New York: Routledge, 1994.

Questions

1. "Don't go to school, the earth might blow up today," says thirteen-year-old Michelle. And "Anna's life," we are told, is "scarcely breathing" – for "she too" is "touched by the thin black cloud" that, "advancing peacefully towards the earth, slowly, soundlessly, in a great silence," would soon "snuff out everything that had lived." For she and Michelle, the threat of apocalypse is certain. Discuss the ways in which this "reign of male terror," manifests within and upon these teenaged bodies, paying particular attention to negotiations of violation, submission and resistance.

2. Both Guislane and Raymond are besieged with guilt and grief at what they perceive as their daughters' inclination towards self-annihilation. At the same time, however, these mothers also feel disgust, aversion, and in several instances, jealousy. Explore the complexities of these mother-daughter relationships.

3 In her discussion of movement in narrative, Nathalie Stephens advocates the idea of "reach" – "a physical motioning in language that seeks to move (forbidden) outside of the many constraints imposed on it" – "a philosophy of reading (and writing) that is concerned less with arriving than it is with experience, writing that is beside language, a movement that is underneath." Discuss the value of this in relation to Blais' narrative approach as she maps the vertiginous geographies of Anna's world.

Of Interest on the Web

http://www.collectionscanada.gc.ca/writers/027005-1000-e.html

http://www.britannica.com/eb/article-9015578/Marie-Claire-Blais

Exile Online Resource

www.ExileEditions.com has a section for the Exile Classics Series, with further resources for all the books in the series.

Exile Classics by Marie-Claire Blais

Coltman, Derek (trans). *A Season in the Life of Emmanuel.*
Toronto: Exile Editions Classics Series, 2008. [Originally
published in French in 1965.]

Coltman, Derek and David Lobdell (trans). *The Manuscripts of
Pauline Archange.* (Includes *Dürer's World*)
Toronto: Exile Editions Classics Series, 2009. [Originally
published in French in 1970.]

Dunlop, Carol (trans). *Deaf to the City.*
Toronto: Exile Editions Classics Series, 2006. [Originally
published in French in 1979.]

Ellenwood, Ray (trans). *Nights in the Underground.*
Toronto: Exile Editions Classics Series, 2006. [Originally
published in French in 1978.]

Fischman, Sheila (trans). *The Wolf.*
Toronto: Exile Editions Classics Series, 2008. [Originally
published in French in 1970.]